TWO SUMMERS

IN NORWAY.

BY THE AUTHOR OF

"THE ANGLER IN IRELAND."

IN TWO VOLUMES.
VOL. II.

LONDON:
SAUNDERS AND OTLEY, CONDUIT STREET.

———

1840.

TWO SUMMERS IN NORWAY.

CHAPTER VIII.

On revisiting the Namsen, in 1839, I reached
my old quarters at Mediaa, by the 11th of
July: and received the most affectionate welcome, not only from my good host Iver, and
his family, but also from all whom I had formerly known, who seemed universally to regard

me as an old friend. I was also glad to see, that both here and at my other quarters on the River, the money spent among them, and the experience they had obtained of an Englishman's requirements, had partly been laid out, as they promised me it should be, in furnishing their houses with many domestic comforts before wanting.

The Namsen was still of a milkyish hue, and daily rising without rain; which proved that the snows had not yet disappeared from the Fjelder where it has its source. However, an English Gentleman, who had anticipated me by a few days, had already caught several Salmon; though none of any size : he reported that the river was full of an unusual number of small Grilse : but at least it was evidently not too early to try the fly.

My expectations of success were much increased by the conviction that I was far better prepared than on my first visit. My previous ignorance of the character of the stream, and the size of the fish, had caused me to fill my books with flies and tackle totally unsuited to the monsters I had to encounter. This summer, I took care to bring with me an abundant store of gigantic flies, made by Evatt, of Warwick-street, and Kelly, of Dublin, as well as some of the largest used on the Tweed for the Spring fishing. I found them all answer well; but those tied by Evatt, having been manufactured under my own superintendence, were, perhaps, the best adapted to the River. It is but justice to an excellent fly-tier to add that they were as unimpeachable for strength, as for beauty. They were most severely tested; and neither the gut nor steel gave way with the heaviest fish: withal, they were as cheap as could be reasonably expected for such an article.

In general, the most brilliant colours were the most successful; such as blood red, bright orange, or brilliant blue, with handsome wings of the golden Pheasant, and other showy feathers. When, however, the water became low and clear, dark colours, *so long as they were really dark, not dingy*, usually answered best. In Salmon fishing, the colours should always be decided; half and half shades, neither one thing nor another, are highly objectionable : the fly ought to have either a well pronounced, and uniform character, or else a marked contrast of colours.

At times, I found a perfectly black body, with jet black hackle, and broad silver twist, with light or even white wings, very killing. A few of the Tweed flies also, in which half the body was black, and the other half bright orange, were occasionally successful : but I lost so many large fish, either by the Scotch hooks breaking, or the gut snapping close to the head, that I latterly seldom employed them.

As I came to the Namsen for the express purpose of killing heavy fish, I used none but flies of the very largest size : and having invariably had better success than any of my countrymen with whom I came in contact on this river (who usually employed much smaller flies) both in the number, and individual size, as well as total weight of fish, I cannot do otherwise than recommend my successors on that noble stream to follow my example. At the same time, this inordinate size of the fly was very unfavourable to hooking small Grilse; which will in some measure account for the disproportion between the rises and the captures recorded in my list.

The line that I found to answer the best, was a silk one well oiled, by Martin Kelly: it ran out and was wound up, more easily, and also was stronger, than the patent mixture of horse-hair and silk, which is preferable where continual casting is required, but is not so well adapted to the Namsen. The objection to the silk line is, that it is heavy, and in wet weather is apt to cling to the rod: but it is not so liable to chafe, or become entangled, as the patent line, and besides takes up less space. I surely need scarcely add that the casting line

must be of the strongest treble gut, the reel
of ample dimensions and single action, the gaff
of wide curve, and firm build. As for the rod,
each Angler has his favourite maker; but I
confess that, after trying many, I have found
none equal to those manufactured by George
Eaton, of Crooked-lane, for perfection of finish,
truth, and durability.

My superior equipments, as well as my
improved acquaintance with the river, justified
my expectation of much greater success than
what I had enjoyed on my former visit. However, many untoward circumstances contributed
to counterbalance these advantages. The summer of 1837 had indeed been so sultry as
generally to prevent my fishing except in the
morning, or evening; whereas in 1839 I could
almost always angle throughout the day. But
then, in the former year there were several
high floods, after each of which the river was
filled with heavy Salmon; while in the latter,
there was but once or twice a slight rise of

water, without which, not even in so copious
a stream as the Namsen, will the larger fish
run up in any quantities. Moreover, on my
first visit I had the river nearly to myself;
whereas I have already mentioned that an
English Angler had arrived before me in 1839,
who continued during the greater part of my
stay: besides which, two other countrymen
occupied the best portion of the river, during
the best of the season.

But still more than this, many of the natives
had taken up angling in the English method.
I have before observed that, though the Norwegians are not endowed with inventive talent,
they show a great turn for imitation: and
either by rowing in the boats with Englishmen,
or by watching them from shore, they had
picked up enough of the art, to annoy us at
least, if not to secure much sport for themselves. Their tackle was of the rudest description: but yet sufficient at least to rise the
most taking fish. If these were small, they

were frequently killed; if they were strong,
away went the flimsy gear: but at all events
the passage of the boats and flies over the
pools, much diminished the chance of any
better Artist who followed them.

I was also grieved to find that not only had
this newly-developed passion for Fly-fishing
made them unusually jealous of their supposed
rights on the River, but also that those who
were not employed as boatmen had begun to
grudge their more favoured neighbours that
were enlisted in the Englishmen's service. The
four orts, or 3s. 4d., which we gave for two
men and a boat, per diem, with a liberal share
of fish and other perquisites, were too great an
object of envy in this poor district. Consequently, all wanted to pull in my boat: and as
I had no idea of being dictated to, in a matter on which my chance of sport so much
depended, as the selection of my Boatmen,
I had some trouble in silencing, I will not
say satisfying, their conflicting claims.

The first year I was on the Namsen, all whom I employed, or to whom I gave fish, expressed the greatest gratitude: this summer, it seemed that those who were excluded took offence, while the others received our guerdon almost as a right. I am inclined to believe that much of this wrong feeling was attributable to the conduct of some Englishmen, in the preceding year, who from an ignorance of the language and customs of the country, had not only fished on the Sabbath, which gave deep offence; but had habitually taken their Fossland boatmen to all parts of the river where they had no shadow of right, and had never made a fair distribution of the Salmon, among the Farmers in whose water they were taken. They consequently left an unfavourable character behind them, except with those who were immediately benefited by their expenditure; and a load of obloquy for their countrymen to fight against. Should this feeling, and the passion for angling increase, the *beaux jours* of the Namsen are past.

The Englishman, to whom I alluded as having preceded me, lodged with my former boatman, Lorenz, and of course employed him: I was therefore compelled to take, in addition to my host's son, a neighbouring farmer, named Johannes Claussen, of Mediaa. He rowed well, and was intelligent enough, but not of a character to please me in other respects: he was also very fond of Angling, and I retained him in my service, more to keep him from mischief, than from affection.

In describing my first visit to the Namsen, I attempted to give some slight account of each day's sport; thinking that such details, however bald, would convey a juster idea of the capabilities of the river, than if I had culled only two or three of the best days, leaving the Reader to imagine that the rest were equally brilliant. However, on this occasion, I shall content myself with a more general description; or only detail those exploits, which seem to deserve especial commemoration.

I have already mentioned the fact of the far greater proportion of small Grilse, which appeared in the river this summer, and the want of floods to induce the large Salmon to run up, until towards the end of my stay. In consequence of this, I had by no means so many opportunities of capturing immense fish, as I had lost on my former visit : but on the other hand, experience had taught me to profit better by such as fell in my way. I had so well drilled my boatmen as to be able to follow the movements of the most violent Salmon, with a short line, and a steady hand : so that if only the hook held, I did not often let him escape, even in the most cramped place.

The morning after my arrival, my countryman having given up to me the water below Mediaa, which he had been fishing for the last week, I sallied forth at an early hour. The upper streams were far too full of snow water : and I saw nothing but a Grilse or two, until I came to Spækkan Pool, above Moe, before honourably mentioned. Here I immediately rose four or five fish, and killed three, one of them of twenty-five pounds, that quite gladdened my eyes, as reminding me of my old friends in this magnificent stream. I rose no other heavy fish; the river appearing to be monopolized by a shoal of Grilse, of four or five pounds' weight.

The next day, I started with the intention of paying my respects to Priest Sörensen at Værum: but was fortunately stopped by a storm of rain, at Spækkan Pool, where the most glorious sport subsequently detained me till the evening. Fresh fish were continually running up from the sea, as was shown by the lice still adhering to many: they seemed to be exclusively of two sizes, small Grilse, or Salmon of about twenty pounds. In this single Pool I rose sixteen fish; and killed ten: of which five were from eighteen to twenty-two pounds, and gave me splendid sport. My total weight this day, with eleven fish, was

137 pounds, the highest figure I had yet attained on the Namsen.

On the following Monday, I gave up this part of the river to my English friend, and tried the Fossland water, where he had totally failed with his small flies. I found indeed the best pools still too high: but in the shallower part of " Fossland Reach," I hooked and killed, after an hour's strong play, a very powerful fish of twenty-eight pounds; besides losing another of nearly equal size, in consequence of not choosing to allow him to run among some dangerous rocks, for which he fought hard, and the hold gave way.

But this was nothing to the success that awaited me in the "Elbow Pool," a favourite spot for large Salmon when the water is high.

Here a fish rose, evidently of great size, but unfortunately missed the fly: and although I tried two or three other beautiful deceptions, I could not induce it to stir again, until an irresistible red fly of Evatt's, tempted it to its destruction. Yet even then, it took not the fly into its mouth; but by good luck I struck the barbed steel into the muscle of the pectoral fin, which afforded as good a hold, though of course not so much command over the fish, as if it had been fixed in the jaw. For the first ten minutes, the monster was highly "indignant of the guile;" shooting up and down and athwart the stream, with a speed extremely difficult to follow: for to attempt to curb him at the first, was entirely out of question.

At length, however, by what appeared to myself and boatmen to be dexterous handling, I succeeded in steering him past all danger into a deep still pool; where I bore upon him with my whole strength, and after several ineffectual struggles, brought him near enough to be gaffed. In a few seconds more it was weighed; when it proved to be over forty pounds, the heaviest I have ever killed on this, or any other river. It was only three feet ten and a half inches in length, that is an inch shorter than the two largest I killed on my former visit; although it exceeded them in weight, by three, and six pounds respectively.

When I saw the huge creature stretched upon the shore, with his deep, thick flanks, and enormously powerful tail and fins, I could scarcely comprehend how I had, in so short a time, baffled his utmost strength, in his native element. For, notwithstanding it was hooked foul, my servant ascertained by his watch, that the fish was landed in exactly half an hour, from the moment of being hooked. Many of inferior size took double the time before they would yield; those of twenty-eight pounds, being usually, according to my experience, the strongest and most active.

I caught one other lively fish of fourteen pounds: but to my infinite annoyance, as I was returning to Mediaa, I perceived a Seal, evidently on his way up the river, in pursuit of the shoal of Salmon that had recently appeared; and the following day, near Værum, another of these unwelcome intruders displayed his bull-dog visage above the water, just as I reached the best Pool, and of course destroyed all my chance of sport.

Leaving my countryman to settle the matter with these arch enemies of the Angler, I resolved on trying what the Fiskum Pools would produce. It was with great satisfaction that I gazed again upon all my well remembered haunts, where I had so enjoyed myself two brief summers before. The Foss was full of water, and in high beauty: and even "Minimum House," bore evidence of having been garnished in expectation of my arrival. But more than all, every one expressed so much gratification at seeing me once more amongst them, that my heart irresistibly warmed to the kindly natives of this wild district.

The renewal of my acquaintance with this part of the River, however, was not so satisfactory in other respects. The Foss Pool was unapproachable from the quantity of water: and instead of finding the other Pools as full of Salmon as I had expected, they seemed to contain hardly any large fish. Nor was this the worst: I had immediate and most disagreeable proof that the passion for Angling had wonderfully extended since I was last here. On reaching the "Boat Pool," I saw it was already preoccupied by a couple of men from Gothland; and either they, or others, regularly fished the best places on every favourable evening.

By far the most annoying of these interlopers was Jacob of Rossætter, who lived close to the splendid Pool I have named after him. The very first day I attempted to fish there, he came down in his boat, and signified to me in most uncivil terms that he expected I should give him up all the fish I might catch, although even by their own customs he was only half owner of the water. And upon my telling him he should have his fair share of what I caught, in the same way as he well knew I treated all the neighbouring Farmers, he proceeded in a very impertinent way to fish the Pool in conjunction with me; a process which he only varied subsequently, by doing the same every day before me.

One evening, however, he was more than usually obnoxious : for, after having spoiled my sport in the lower Pools, directly that he observed me on my return homewards, he pushed on before me, to anticipate me in my own Boat Pool, where he knew I always took my latest cast. Seeing his object, I allowed him plenty of time; thinking he would become tired, and depart I misjudged my man ! On my arrival at that immense Pool, he instantly left the upper part where he was fishing, and bearing down upon me, in the most insolent manner, swung his boat round actually upon my line. It was well for him that I was not a man of war; or the indignant remonstrances

I showered on him in my best Norsk, would have been replaced by more intelligible indications of my feelings. I, however, took care to let every one hear of his conduct, as well as my opinion of it: and as all the respectable neighbours, including my good friend the Priest, sided with me, Jacob was eventually shamed into better behaviour. He attempted to excuse himself by alleging (whether truly or falsely, I know not) that two English officers, the previous summer, had daily fished his water, without giving him any share of the Salmon; and that he expected I meant to do the same.

The only day that I had any sport to compensate for these annoyances, was the last I spent at Fiskum on this occasion: when, after shooting some Capercailzie in the morning, I took my boat into the Foss Pool, which I had not been able to try before. There was still so large a body of water as to render this a difficult, and with any other than such ex-

cellent boatmen as I had, a dangerous operation. The thundering river that dashed over
the lofty Fall threatened every moment to
sweep us away, as we shot across the rapid
torrent. However we accomplished it in safety,
although drenched with the heavy spray, as
much as if we had been exposed to the pelting
of the most pitiless storm.

From a rock that advanced as near to the
Fall as I could possibly penetrate, I rose an
immense fish in the very breakers, I am quite
confident not less than forty pounds in weight.
It was, without doubt, the wildest spot in which
I ever hooked a large fish ; and he proved the
wildest of his tribe. He plunged at once into
the very centre of the cataract, apparently with
an intention of sounding its lowest depths ;
my line was nearly run out, yet I scarcely
knew where the fish was, when I suddenly saw
him springing amidst the foaming surge, more
than 100 yards from me.

He next made the most desperate efforts to

escape into the lower Pool, whither I could not follow him, except by shooting a rapid of so perilous a character, that I preferred holding him by main force, notwithstanding all his struggles. I expected each instant that some part of my rod or line would break; but so good was my tackle, that it bore the enormous pressure upon it, without giving way: and I had already brought the monster some distance up the violent stream, and he was showing evident symptoms of weakness, when after half an hour's most splendid play, the hook came out of his mouth, and he escaped.

Without wasting time in useless regrets, I returned to the same rock, and at the first cast hooked another fine Salmon, which I at once saw was some dozen pounds less than the one I had just lost. Yet did he look most magnificent, from the elevated spot where I stood, as he darted through the eddying foam, to seize the fly. He pursued exactly the same tactics as his predecessor; and when, finally, he persisted, in spite of all my efforts, in rushing down the impetuous stream, I resolved at all hazards to follow him, not choosing to lose two such fine fish, without a brave effort at least.

We were dreadfully knocked about, and nearly swamped in the attempt: however, we safely entered "Karnen's Pool" with the Salmon, whom I then easily killed; and he weighed upwards of twenty-eight pounds. I can scarcely conceive it possible to enjoy finer sport than I had with these two fish: more vigorous Salmon, or a wilder spot to play them in, I never saw. It will be seen by my list that I also caught six smaller fish, without even trying below the Boat Pool.

A day or two after my return to Mediaa, some heavy rain slightly flooded the river, and was immediately followed by the appearance of numerous large fish. I was fortunate enough on two successive days to encounter these shoals on their progress upwards, at two most excellent spots: on the 27th, at a bend of the

river, near Værum, called Gunhild's Bjerg;
and on the 29th, at my favourite Pool of Spækkan. It is of the greatest importance, in fishing the Namsen, to take care, whenever from
the state of the water Salmon may be expected
to run up, to be upon one of the best Pools.
They rest in such places for a short time, during
which they take the fly well; and then rapidly
pass up, leaving the streams quite deserted,
which a few hours before swarmed with fish.

I had a good example of this at Gunhild's
Bjerg. I could plainly observe the Salmon
spring up the Rapid at its lower end: again
and again I fished the water over, rising fresh
fish each time. I altogether rose eighteen within
three or four hours, several of them large and
very strong: I killed two of twenty-eight
pounds, and two of nearly twenty pounds each,
besides five Grilse. But when I tried the Pool
again in the evening, after having dined with
my kind friends at Værum, not a Salmon was
to be seen; all had passed up.

On the 29th I had an equally good morning's
sport at Spækkan, of exactly the same character;
only that the rain came down so heavily, and
so much discoloured the water, as to drive
me home before the day was half spent, and
while numbers of fresh Salmon, of the largest
size, were running up each moment into the
Pool.

It was unfortunate for my piscatory success
at this period, that I had previously arranged
to spend the next few days with Priest Sörensen,
at Værum: for few fish remained in this lower
part of the River, and the weather became so
hot, as quite to disincline those few to move at
the fly. However, I was amply recompensed
by the friendly society of this very amiable
family, from each of whom I received marks of
kindness calculated to impress me with the
most favourable recollections of the Norwegian
character.

The Glebe-house of Værum is not worthy
of its inmates, being both insufficiently small,

and out of repair. But its situation is picturesque, at a sudden bend of the Namsen, occasioned by the lofty Steen Fjeld, which stands
rudely across its course; while other more
distant and finely broken mountains form a
perfect amphitheatre around. The precipitous
range of the Steen Fjeld so overhangs Værum
to the eastward, as entirely to exclude all sight
of the sun, during thirteen weeks of the winter, when that luminary rises but a short way
above the horizon. How inexpressibly joyous
must be the sight of the long lost orb, when
he first peers above the rocky summit! the
well remembered day of his reappearance is
anxiously watched, and obsérved as a fête in
the neighbourhood.

On my return to Fiskum, I had very excellent sport, as may be partly gathered from my
list. There was not a day that I did not catch
many large fish, besides the many more that
I hooked and played: and in such wild places!
I several times tried the wildest of all, the

Foss Pool: but it was not until August 12th,
that I was enabled by the gradual falling of
the water to fish any considerable portion of
it; when I enjoyed far the most splendid
day's sport I can ever hope to have to record.
I began well: I had scarcely commenced,
when, off a rock in the Boat Pool, I hooked,
and after long play killed, a beautifully shaped
fish of thirty-four pounds: and soon after,
another of twenty-four pounds near the same
spot, as also a third of eleven pounds. I had
already had a good day's sport: but in the
rapid stream between the Foss and Karnen's
Pools, (which I have named, "the Foss Rapid,") I rose several fish, of which I fortunately
killed the largest, weighing thirty-three pounds,
besides a fine Salmon of eighteen pounds, and
a Grilse.

We then with great difficulty worked our
frail bark up into the Foss Pool; and at the
risk of shipping a perilous quantity of water,
proceeded to fish as well as I could a small

extent of flat water, by the side of the boiling torrent. Never in my life have I encountered such wild water! Scarcely had I cast 'my fly into the most likely spot, when an enormous Salmon took it, but being slightly hooked, soon escaped. A minute afterwards, a monster of similar size dashed through the glancing waves; and I instantly felt he was firmly hooked. In another moment he was in the midst of the Fall: baffled there, he rushed up and down, with a determination of purpose, but irregularity of course, that made it very difficult to retain a correct hold upon him. I could not stand in the boat that danced on the bounding breakers: scarcely could I see or hear, so blinded was I with the spray, so deafened with the cataract's eternal roar.

At last he made down the stream as if to quit the Pool; and we prepared to follow him through the dangerous Rapid already described. However, it seemed that his courage failed him, and he took refuge behind a deeply sunk rock, from which it required much positive labour and strength to dislodge him. At length, he was compelled to yield; and on being landed, was found to weigh thirty-seven pounds; but though therefore not the heaviest, he was by nearly an inch the longest Salmon I ever killed, measuring rather over four feet.

In the same spot, I afterwards caught two beautiful, fresh run Salmon of twenty-four, and eighteen pounds each: and hooked two other heavy fish, one of which (certainly not under thirty pounds in weight) I played for a considerable time; when he eventually broke the line by entangling it round a rock, a misfortune not to be wondered at in so dangerous a place. And, finally, I concluded this brilliant day by landing a pretty Salmon of ten pounds, and a small Grilse; making a total weight of 216 pounds with eleven fish. A gratifying total under any circumstances: but when the individual size of the Salmon is further considered, and still more the character of the water in which they were killed, I am almost tempted to doubt whether any Salmon fisher ever enjoyed a more glorious day's sport.

The weather about this time became very much broken : the 13th of August that I fished down to Fossland was cold and raw, as winter; and in the course of the night it froze suffi- ciently to blacken the potatoe tops. The fol- lowing day was little bettter : but being fortu- nately able to reach the Foss Pool in the after- noon, I killed there four magnificent Salmon, which averaged twenty-six pounds each; and afforded me great sport. The next day I was also very successful, catching seven fish, which weighed together ninety-seven pounds; not- withstanding that I was very unlucky in losing several good Salmon, apparently without any just cause.

And this was the last good day's sport that I was destined to have upon the Namsen: for during the two following days that I remained at Fiskum, the water rapidly fell, and the fish seemed simultaneously to quit this part of the River. There was still a far larger body of water than I ever saw in the Tweed; yet I had undeniable evidence that the Salmon, even at this early season, returned to the sea. Not only did they suddenly disappear from all the upper Pools, but frequently, while fishing, I observed Salmon, that from their size and colour I could not possibly mistake, jump once or twice at the higher end of a pool, which they appeared to have but just entered; then soon after towards the middle, and again spring at the bottom, within the course of a few minutes: after which I saw no more of them.

On August 17, I was able to fish over the greater part of the Foss Pool; but only saw two Grilse jump: I rose none there with the fly. It seemed that after ascertaining the impossibility of surmounting the cataract, the majority had dropped down the river, as soon as they found the water begin to lower. The few Salmon that remained, moreover, took the

Much better is the Overhalden River, up which Salmon ascend as far as Flasnæs; though not in any considerable numbers. I several times intended to try it, from mere curiosity, although aware I could expect no sport to compensate for what I gave up on the Namsen: but circumstances, unnecessary to mention, prevented me.

The Sportsman, who is fond of shooting, will find more to occupy his attention. On my first visit to this district, I saw little game except wild ducks, and golden plover: but the next time I was there, I greatly improved my larder by the discovery that there were a great number of Ryper (or Ptarmigan) on the mountains, as well as Capercailzie, and Hjerper (*Tetrao Bonasia*, or the hazel hen) in the forests. The latter is the most delicately flavoured bird I know. The breast has not the layer of brown flesh usual to other game birds, but is of the purest white throughout. This is accounted for by an old Norwegian tradition, to the effect that there was originally one enormously large Hjerpe, on which all the other birds pounced, and partly devoured, whence they obtained the layer of white flesh they possess next the breast ; and their poor victim became dimi- nished to its present proportions. They are very tame, at least here, where they are so little disturbed; and when roused from their feeding ground, fly up into the neighbouring trees, gazing stupidly at the intruder.

I always made a point of allowing my boat- men a couple of hours' sleep after their mid-day meal; and while they were taking 'their sièsta, I dived into the nearest pine forest, and rarely returned without either Hjerper, or young Capercailzie: I saw some old Cocks, but they escaped me. I had no dog: but my English friend before mentioned occasionally took the Fjeld, with a brace of Setters ; and generally killed from five to ten brace of Ptarmigan, be- sides other Game.

By far his greatest exploit, however, was the

slaughter of a Bear, which had killed a cow, about three miles from the Gaard where he lodged: whereupon he went up to the spot the next evening; and on the beast's returning, as he expected, to taste its dainty prey, he fortunately succeeded in disabling it at the first shot. It proved to be an old, and not very large female: but the courage with which our countryman lay in his solitary ambush, within twenty-five yards of the ferocious brute, much enhanced the natives' idea, not only of his individual, but of the national bravery.

There were many other bears known to be in the neighbourhood: insomuch, that I doubt not a man like Mr. Lloyd, properly equipped for this chace, would have great success, and would confer a valuable benefit on the inhabitants, who are dreadfully afraid of Mr. Bruin. Wolves are also abundant, particularly in the mountains near the Sætters; and still more in the vicinity of the Lapps and their Reindeer. They are so shy, that I never actually saw one:

but thrice we observed the fresh print of their
feet on our path to the Boat Pool : and during
my stay many dogs were devoured by them.

Occasionally, in searching for other game, I
flushed a Woodcock: but though they undoubtedly breed in this country, I do not believe
they are very common. Besides five or six
species of Ducks that frequent the Namsen, I
every day saw numbers of the Northern Diver ;
of which I shot a few. And to complete my
brief list of the wild birds of this district, I will
only mention that in addition to the Fishing
Eagles, which were usually to be seen near
Fossland, I frequently observed Eagles of the
largest kind soaring above us; and on one
occasion I saw a pair, I believe of Golden
Eagles, perched for the night on the face of
a perpendicular crag near the Long Reach,
which, though screaming at me all the while,
allowed me to approach within a hundred yards.
Singular enough too, an immense specimen of
the large Norway Owl, from the summit of the

same cliff, kept hooting at me, while attempting to creep within shot, across the crackling wood.

But much the most interesting animals that fell under my observation were the Lemmings. This singular little species of the genus *Mus*, is confined, I believe, to Scandinavia, and some Northern portions of Russia. Its appearance is periodical; some say it appears every seventh, others every tenth year. It also seems to be capricious in its choice of residence, as whole provinces are infested with it, while in the intermediate districts not one is visible. On my former Tour through Norway, I did not see a single Lemming; this year, 1839, they abounded in certain parts, but not every where.

I have mentioned that I saw the first on the Fille Fjeld, and Sogne Fjeld: there were none in Romsdalen, or on the Dovre Fjeld, while the Western shores of the Mjösen swarmed with them. From that point I saw none until I reached Steenkjær, where there were a few, which rapidly increased until I reached Nummedal, where they were in thousands. Naturalists account for their periodical appearance by supposing that they inhabit the most retired mountains, until they have multiplied beyond the means of subsistence, when they become gregarious, and descend into the plains. There most of them perish: the few that return, with those that have remained in the mountains, repeat the same process, after a certain time, with the same result.

The natives have a much simpler, if not so scientific explanation of the phænomenon, being convinced that they drop from the clouds in a thunder storm. I have talked with many who had been accustomed to traverse the mountains all their lives, and who assured me they had never seen a single Lemming in any intermediate season. I suspect, however, that they may be always found at least in the Northern portion of the Kjölen Chain which

separates Norway from Sweden. It is from
this direction that they appear originally to
come; in great numbers certainly, but not in
such dense masses, as some old books would
lead one to imagine. Though there may be
many hundreds within the space of an acre, it
is seldom you see more than two or three together; much oftener, they are single.

They are said universally to travel westwards;
and no obstacle stops them; not only will they
paddle across such rapid streams as the Namsen,
but even over salt water Fjords ten miles in
width. Yet they do not seem well adapted for
swimming: their legs are very short, their feet
extremely small and delicate, without any web.
Their colour is a rich brown, broadly striped with
black on the back, and softening into light fawn
colour on the belly. Their bodies are plump;
their tail not half an inch in length; their heads
rather short and thick, so that altogether they
have much more the look of a Guinea pig than
of a rat. They have, however, the rat's teeth; and

if attacked, stand up on their hind legs, squeaking shrilly all the time, and springing at their foe, just like the rat.

They are very fierce, when first caught, but some that I brought to England, soon became sufficiently tame to allow themselves to be handled: and very pretty little creatures they were. I carried eight of them about with me for several weeks in a small box; and notwithstanding the rough usage to which they were necessarily exposed on the road, they maintained excellent health. I fed them chiefly on brown bread and vegetables, with occasionally a little meat, or fish: in fact, they would eat any thing. Unfortunately, one of the last nights I spent in Norway, six of them escaped through the negligence of my servant, when I could no longer replace them. The other two I consigned to the Zoological Gardens, Regent's Park, in the best apparent health: but they both died within a week, through some mismanagement. These singular animals are usually preceded on their migrations by an Arvicola, called here the Blue Lemming. It is of a sooty blue colour, and altogether much more resembles a very large mouse, than the Lemming: its tail is much longer, and its motions infinitely quicker: it is also far rarer.

The Lemmings do great mischief in the fields, devouring every thing that falls in their way: but they have many enemies, biped, quadruped, and winged. I was even informed, upon authority that I cannot possibly question, that the Reindeer not only kills them, but is very fond of eating them! That an herbivorous and ruminating animal should show a penchant for such food, seems passing strange: but in addition to other witnesses, Priest Sörensen, a gentleman of unimpeachable veracity, and enjoying the best opportunities of observation during his annual visits to the Lapps' Chapels, positively assured me that when a Reindeer observes a Lemming at any distance, he runs to it, strikes it dead with a blow of his fore-foot, and instantly swallows it whole! This may appear strange to others, as it did to me: I can only say that I could scarcely have better evidence, short of actual sight, than I obtained of this singular fact.

A still greater enemy to the Farmer in certain districts, this year, was a perfectly smooth caterpillar, of a dark olive colour, and about three quarters of an inch in length. In many vallies to the North of Trondhjem, it appeared in incredible numbers, during the early part of the summer, and completely laid bare not only the meadows, but also the young corn fields. Old people told me they remembered the appearance of a similar plague, some thirty years ago.

But there remains one still greater enemy to the "Landed Interest," with which the farmer of Nummedal has to contend; that is, the early frosts, which too often destroy all his hopes in a single night. This was the case in 1838: and indeed had happened, more or less, on all the higher Farms for the last four years. No wonder therefore that the frost which occurred on August 13th of this year, (1839,) caused great consternation; it blackened many of the potato fields; and two or three nights afterwards the barley was frostbitten in exposed situations, which induced many to cut their corn quite green, rather than run the risk of losing it all.

Poor People! they were generally suffering privations, such as, even in Ireland, would be considered grievous. Scarcely any of the better farmers could afford to eat pure barley bread, without any mixture of fir bark: and very many were compelled to live on bark bread alone! The stock of the district being exhausted, all who could scrape the money together, sent some of the family to purchase corn, after the patriarchal fashion, at the nearest markets along the sea coast. They seldom could obtain it at a less distance than seventy or eighty miles: the price was very high, and the quality indifferent: while the toil of poling up such a stream as the Namsen with a heavily laden boat, may be imagined.

Under such circumstances, even the little addition to their stock of food, which my rod and gun afforded, was an object of some consequence: still more so, was the money I disbursed among them. Even the better class of farmers, though able to live in tolerable comfort upon the produce of their land in ordinary seasons, have little or no opportunity of realizing money. They have nothing to sell; and there is no one to buy; forasmuch as each of their countrymen supplies himself, in the same manner, that they do, with the three great necessaries of human existence, "Fire, food, and clothes." The small sums, therefore, that I distributed to my hosts and boatmen, were an object of competition, which, as we have seen, occasioned some bickering at first: nay, I was even favoured with a sort of Round Robin on the subject from four of the farmers of Grong. However, by just dealing and the powerful assistance of my friend the Priest, I eventually succeeded in allaying this feeling, so as to part from all not only on the most amicable terms, but apparently with deep regret.

From the best information I could obtain in Christiania, I believe that, according to law, Angling is on the same footing as shooting, which is perfectly unrestricted throughout Norway. I was assured by the highest authority that no one can prevent any other from fishing in a boat, or even from landing, except upon enclosed and cultivated ground. But though I believe this to be the undoubted law of the kingdom, the Bönder have established a law among themselves, to which the stranger must, for his own sake, pay some deference.

Each proprietor considers he is entitled to the fishery of the river opposite his farm: and I respected this supposed right so far as always to present one half of my booty to the farmer

in whose fishery it was caught: the other moiety
I reserved for myself, boatmen, and host.   But
when they wished me also to take my rowers
invariably from the Gaards opposite to which I
angled, I decidedly refused.   From Fiskum
down to Værum there are thirty-seven proprietors on the water : and as I have shown how
much depends on the discipline of the boat,
it never would answer to be constantly chang-
ing your men, just after teaching them their
duty.

I should, however, most strongly recommend
any of my countrymen who may follow me to
the Namsen, invariably to select their boatmen
from the principal proprietors of the part of the
river they fish : thus, from Fiskum, while angling in the upper part ; from Fossland, when
in the centre ; from Grong or Mediaa, when on
the lower portion : and if they remain any
length of time, it will be as well occasionally to
change their men.

I think I have mentioned the established

tariff to be four marks, (*orts*, they are called
in the North) per diem, or 3*s*. 4*d*. for a boat
with two rowers. Moreover, I made it a
rule to give a dollar (four shillings English)
for every Salmon over thirty pounds, or for
a total weight of 100 pounds caught in one
day: which gave my men an interest in my
success, without materially increasing the expenses of the Tour. At the various houses
where I lodged, I gave half a dollar a day for
my lodging, cooking, barley bread, potatoes,
butter, and milk: every thing else I provided:
and as my hosts also got a good share of the
fish, and often pulled in my boat, they were
abundantly satisfied.

It is not more than forty years since the
first potatoes were introduced as a curiosity
into this district; they are now universal, and
in general excellent. The butter is by far the
sweetest and most luscious I ever met with anywhere: and latterly my breakfasts were much
improved by mountain strawberries of exqui-

site flavour, and the far-famed Moltebær before
described.

I linger still upon the Namsen, though I
much fear the reader who is only acquainted
with that noble River through these pages, will
hardly partake of the enthusiasm with which
I look back on the happy days I spent upon its
banks. Every thing contributed to render
them amongst the happiest, for which I am
indebted to my passion for Angling. The excellence of my sport, the grandeur of the
scenery, the primitive and novel mode of life
of the natives, with the uninterrupted health
and lightsome spirits I enjoyed, made those
six weeks glide imperceptibly away with unwelcome rapidity. It seemed but a few days
since I had witnessed the crops emerge from
the ground; and already the sickle was busy
in every field. Autumn had evidently arrived;
and the almost nightly frosts told that Winter
was rapidly advancing from his Northern Halls.
Therefore after again visiting my most kind

and amiable friends at Værum, where a large
party was assembled for the annual Visitation,
I bade a final adieu to this King of Salmon
Rivers on the 23rd of August, and returned by
the Snaasen Vand to Trondhjem.

CHAPTER IX.

Route from Trondhjem to Molde—Örkedal—Surendal—Ferries
on the Western Fjords—Delays and difficulties—Beauty of
scenery—A midnight Voyage—Romsdalen—Magnificent
prospects—A couple of days' Angling—Another excursion to the Fjeld—Great success—Three Reindeer shot—
Upper part of Romsdalen—Traditions of Colonel Sinclair
—An overturn—Lake Lessöe—Guldbrandsdal—Return to
Christiania.

I HAD heard so much of the beauty of the
Western Fjords, and of the picturesque grandeur of Romsdalen, that I determined to vary
my route, on my last return from Trondhjem to
Christiania, by taking that line, in preference
to either of the more direct roads by Röraas,
or the Dovre Fjeld, both of which I had already
seen.   In addition to the novelty of this Western route, I knew from the experience of two
friends whom I met on the Namsen, that very
fair Salmon fishing might be enjoyed at certain

seasons in the Rauma Elv: while the only drawback was the annoyance to be expected at the many Ferries across the Fjords.

I left Trondhjem for, I fear, the last time, on August 28th, in weather that promised better for the Angler, than the Tourist: it had rained hard during the night; and the heavens were still charged with dark, heavy clouds. I soon quitted the great Southern Road, and crossed an arm of the Trondhjem Fjord, into which the Guul discharges its waters. I heard here, as at all the Northern rivers, that the Salmon had never been so scarce as this summer. In the Nid hardly any fish had been taken; insomuch that the price at Trondhjem had risen to 5d. and 6d. a pound for fresh, and 7d. or 8d. for smoked Salmon.

After leaving the Fjord, the road traverses a mountainous district, covered with fir forests; in the midst of which I came upon a considerable Lake that had every appearance of being well adapted for Angling: I was told there

were plenty of trout in it, but I could not
learn any thing positive as to their size, and
fly fishing had never been practised on it. I
next crossed some high, and very poor ground,
where the crops had been entirely destroyed
by the early frosts, and the inhabitants appeared to be in a most miserable condition.
A long and steep descent brought me into
Örkedal, or the Valley of the Örke, the same
river which I had crossed much higher up, at
Bjerkager, on my way over the Dovre Fjeld.

I observed here the same immense terraces
of alluvial matter, rising one above the other,
which are so commonly seen in the Norwegian
Vallies, that descend from the loftier mountains; and which all attest the same fact of
the water having stood at successively diminishing levels, (all above the present level of the
existing rivers and lakes,) during very considerable periods; for no lesser time could
suffice for the water to wear down the very
hard rocks over which it flows, and deposit such

an enormously thick mass of detritus, as we see here, for instance, and in Værdal. In consequence of this rich deposit, the lower part of Örkedal is remarkably fertile and well cultivated. It has also the charms of a happy combination of hill and wood; which rapidly assume grander features on advancing up the course of the stream.

I took the road on the Western side of the river, as being shorter and less hilly than the other: and at Moe, I was so pleased with the scenery and the appearance of the people, that I was easily persuaded to remain a day for the purpose of trying the Örke. I was well aware that a few Salmon at least ascend this river to a Foss some way above Bjerkager; and it could not be in better order, so that I expected some tolerable sport. Early the next morning, I commenced at a beautiful Pool about a mile above Moe; and fished carefully down for four or five miles. There was a succession of most unexceptionable pools and streams, the day was favourable, and the water in excellent trim; nevertheless, I did not see the slightest sign of a Salmon; and came to the conclusion that at this season there could scarcely be one, in this part of the Örke. I caught but a single white trout, and two or three small river trout.

The natives agreed in assuring me that a couple of months earlier, there had been a good many fish in the water, but that they had now run up higher. They, however, allowed that their numbers had greatly diminished of late years; for which they could not account: but I endeavoured to impress upon them that this fact was very easily explained by their having latterly placed weirs across the entire course of the river, which in ordinary states of the water, prevent any Salmon whatever from passing. This is not only contrary to an express law, but must eventually destroy the best Salmon river; I suspect also that the water from some copper works, about two or three miles above Moe, may contribute

to the extirpation of the fish; as I observed
that the river below them was quite red, whereas higher up it was clear as crystal. Whatever
may be the cause, it is at any rate very evident
that the Örke is not worthy of detaining an
Angler for even a day from better streams.
Hares and Hjerper are tolerably numerous in
this neighbourhood; and at a distance of seven
miles is a considerable mountain Lake, which
contains (as I was assured) very large trout,
and an abundance of Char.

I have said that the scenery around Moe is
extremely picturesque: above, it becomes much
more savage. The valley contracts into a wild
ravine, which hardly allows space enough for
the imprisoned river to force its tumultuous
way: and from the point where I quitted it,
some twelve or fifteen miles from Moe, I could
see that for some distance at least, its deep and
noisy path lay through the same grand gorges,
opening occasionally into short, isolated glens,
of more peaceful character.

The valley of Surendal, into which I now
passed, is far from being so picturesque as that
of Örkedal; though there are in its long course
many scenes to please the lover of mountains.
I have, however, every reason to believe that
its river is much better supplied with Salmon;
as at each of the stations I heard of their
nightly catching several fish with nets.   Whether it may be good for the Angler I cannot
say; as I believe no one has ever tried it, and
my bad success on the Örke determined me to
waste no more time at this season. I can vouch
for there being many tempting streams and
pools, particularly about Haandstad: but at
each of them I also observed nets suspiciously
hung up to dry, which may doubtless interfere
much with fly fishing: and in the upper part,
are the same sort of weirs I reprobated on the
Örke.   In the hills on the Eastern side of the
valley are numerous lakes, full of Char; which
are caught either in the autumn, when they
resort to the shallows to spawn; or in the win-

ter, by making a hole in the ice. A little below Haandstad, the river becomes too wide and
still for Angling.

Surendal debouches into a considerable Fjord,
which extends about thirty miles seawards,
to Christiansund; besides branching out many
miles, in the other direction, into the bosom
of the mountains. My object, however, was
to cross it, a distance of about fourteen miles :
and as it was the first Fjord of any magnitude
that I had attempted to pass with carriages on
board, I felt not a little anxious as to the
feasibility of the operation, with such slight
craft, as I had hitherto seen. I soon found it
would be impossible to convey both carrioles
in the same boat : and I, therefore, despatch-
ed one carriage immediately after my arrival,
with three men and a lighter bark : while I
ordered the largest boat they had, and five
rowers, to be ready for myself early the next
morning.

These Ferries across the wider Fjords are a

sad annoyance to the Tourist in exploring the
magnificent scenery of the Western coast of
Norway.   In bad weather they are impassable,
without great risk : and at the best, are attended, not only with great additional expense,
but with anxiety, trouble, and damage illimit-
able.   It is impossible to calculate the time,
that may be required, so as to despatch a For-
bud for any distance: and without it, the delay
in obtaining men and boats would peril the
temper of the most patient of mortals.

At each Fjord the wheels must be taken off
even a light Carriole; which not merely occasions much trouble, but also much mischief in
the various shipments and unshipments.   All
must help; as the natives are very far from
being expert or intelligent in these arrangements : and then master as well as man must
find as comfortable a berth as he can among
the greasy wheels, or well tarred boards; keep-
ing always a sharp eye to windward, in case it
blows at all, to avoid the splashing waves.

The boats, of whatever size, are universally of the same light build, before described; entirely of fir, pointed and somewhat raised at both ends. Each man pulls a pair of small-feathered oars, except the steersman, who rows with one hand, while with the other he manages a very long-handled rudder. I cannot say that my experience justifies me in calling the Norwegians hard rowers: on the contrary, they take it remarkably easily, and are as glad as any of their fraternity for an excuse of the slightest breeze to hoist a sail.

This much in fine weather: but in stormy weather the traveller may be confined for days in the very miserable pot houses that supply the place of Inns along the coast. Even at Surendalsören, the place of embarkation for two such considerable towns as Christiansund and Molde, the accommodations were both scanty and bad, and the provisions little better; set off by the usual ancient fish-like smell, the least agreeable accompaniment of the seaside.

However, the weather, which had been threat-
ening, changed most unexpectedly, and the
next morning's sun rose in glorious majesty.
How soon does the human mind, when backed
with youth and health, shake off its cares, and
spring at once from zero to contentment's point!
The previous evening, I had been wet, cold,
cast down by the discouraging state of the weather, the unknown perils of the voyage, the
discomforts of " mine own Inn :" but to-day
all was bright and cheering, and my spirits rose
proportionably, to greet and enjoy the rich display of God's creation that awaited me.

Volumes of light mist yet remained, the records of the preceding day's storm : and as they
floated up the dark glens, or curled round the
base of the projecting mountains, under the
influence of the breeze and sun, they added to
scenery, in itself highly grand and beautiful,
those thousand accidents of light and shade,
which any one, who has wandered through a
mountain country, must remember to have

made the deepest impression on his own mind, though the most incapable of transmission, by description to another.

As the mists cleared away, we reached the middle of the passage, whence we commanded three several arms of the Fjord : and I now saw we were surrounded by lofty snowy ranges that towered far above the dark cliffs that immediately enclosed the waters of the Fjord. Those in the direction of Sundalen and Romsdalen, whither I was bound, exhibited especial grandeur of outline and elevation ; and at once satisfied me as to the noble character of the mountain district I was approaching.-

So favourable had been our little voyage, that we reached our place at Vaagöen (fourteen miles from Surendalsören) in a couple of hours : we then harnessed the ponies that awaited us, and rattled over the narrow Isthmus to the station of Bække, on the next Fjord. Here I was made practically aware of some of the *désagremens* attending the navigation of these

arms of the sea. Not expecting to make so
rapid progress, I had ordered the boatmen to
be ready two hours later than the time I
actually arrived: and as they lived at a considerable distance, it was impossible to hasten
them. I had therefore nothing else to do,
but stroll, with as much patience as I might,
along the adjoining shore; while my servant
repaired some serious injury which one of the
carriages had suffered at the last debarkation.

The prospect was such as might well soothe
a more troubled spirit than mine was. It
would be difficult to imagine a more secluded
and tranquil situation, amid scenery on so
large and grand a scale. A beautifully circular
bay, about two miles in breadth, formed a sort
of offshoot from the parent Fjord, which was
seen in the distance branching right and left.
The encircling mountains were lofty and finely
shaped; but though occasionally descending
with steep cliffs into the water, they more frequently swept down with graceful curve, so as

to admit of vegetation high up their verdant
sides, and to afford a secure resting place at
their feet to a few scattered hamlets.

In the midst of this retired scenery stood a
Church, with a Manse attached to it; both, of
a size and consequence that scarcely appeared
proportionate to the scanty population visible
within the extensive amphitheatre I commanded. When I learned that the incumbent
was son of Bishop Bygge, and brother to the
very talented Rector of the Latin School at
Trondhjem, I could not help pitying a man of
his acquirements and education, being so shut
out from the converse of kindred minds, as he
must necessarily be.

Yet even in the cursory survey I took, I
could observe many evidences of the advantage
derived from the presence of a superior person, in the wildest spot. There was a regularly
enclosed garden, (so unusual an appendage to
a Norwegian house,) in which were various
vegetables and fruit trees. The adjoining

fields exhibited a much better state of agricul-
ture, than I had lately seen; while a wellbred
English sow, just imported, showed Priest
Bygge's wish to improve the native breed, of
which it is little to say that it is by far the
worst and ugliest I ever met with. I doubt
not that his exertions to cultivate the minds,
and improve the hearts, of his parishioners,
are at least as energetic and useful. At length
the boatmen arrived, not many minutes after
their time; greatly to the relief of the drunken
old landlord of Bække, who had cunningly
put his clocks half an hour back, lest I should
insert a complaint at their want of punctuality.
Then the boat had to be launched, the oars
to be found, the carriages to be embarked,
various preparations and squabbles to be
adjusted: so that, in short, three precious
hours were lost, and alas! the breeze, which
had hitherto been so favourable, completely
died away; and consequently, we had to pull
to Eidsören, (a distance of eight miles,) in

an overloaded boat, with five men who had
been working hard all the previous morning,
beneath a scorching sun, and a sultry atmo-
sphere. It took us three hours to reach Eidsören, where not having ordered horses I was
again greatly delayed. The distance across
the Isthmus, to Eidsvog on the Lange Fjord,
being only five or six miles, I preferred walking; and just reached it, as Peder came up
with the carriages.

The disasters I had previously encountered
were, however, nothing in comparison with
those that awaited me here. Not a soul was at
home; and when at last we ferreted out the
Skydskaffer, who was cutting corn a couple of
miles off, we found that no ten-oared boat
was at the station, the person bound to supply
such, having illegally taken it away to a fishery.
There was an eight-oared boat, belonging to a
Priest, on the opposite shore : but when I sent
to him for the loan of it, (to which I was entitled
by law,) he returned for answer in a couple of

hours, that he should want it the next day to go to a distant church, and therefore could not let me have it.

By this time the shades of evening had closed in, and a number of peasants returning from their harvest work, had collected around me, from whom I could obtain nothing but commiseration—no assistance. As, however, it was totally impossible to stay where I was, (there being no place to sleep at, and absolutely nothing to eat, not even butter and barley cake) I eventually persuaded three men to take me and my carriole, down the Fjord to Alfarnæs, in the largest boat we could obtain, which was but a small three-oar. It was totally insufficient for the purpose, in any except the finest weather; but as the night, though dark as Erebus, promised to be perfectly calm, I did not hesitate to trust myself in it, leaving Peder to follow when and how he best could.

There seemed something adventurous in thus launching forth into the bosom of the black

night, on a midnight voyage of fourteen or
fifteen miles, over an unknown Fjord, in a frail
bark, with perfect strangers. I wrapped myself up in my cloak in as comfortable a position
as I could assume between the wheels of my
carriole : but the strangeness of my situation
contributed, still more than the uncomfortable-
ness of my posture, to drive sleep from my
eyelids. I never witnessed a darker night: we
could not see distinctly the length of our boat,
so as to render steering impossible* to any but
the most practised native : and I shall never
forget the effect produced by the cottage lights
dotted like indistinct stars upon the sides of
the unseen mountains, at perfectly indistinguishable distances. Every now and then we
crossed lateral arms of the Fjord, or glens in
the line of coast, at the head of which I could
just make out, in " the palpable obscure," the
mysterious outline of snowy peaks, that perhaps looked all the more impressive for the
murky darkness in which they were enveloped.

The morning broke finely, as we approached our goal, and disclosed a wide expanse of the Fjord on which Molde is situated, with some apparently high snow mountains to the Southwest. We soon after reached Alfarnæs, where we knocked the people up, and got some coffee, which greatly refreshed myself and men. They were good, honest fellows, with whom I was much pleased, both for having helped me out of my difficulties when their fellows shrank from the task, as well as for the cheerfulness, steadiness, and skill, with which they had accomplished our nocturnal voyage.

As soon as I could obtain a steed for my carriole, I started for Torvig, where a short Ferry leads across the Fjord, to Veblungsnæs, a small village at the entrance to Romsdalen. During the latter part of this stage, I had ample opportunity for appreciating this scenery, so little visited, though so much vaunted, and to view which I had encountered so many annoyances. I confess that I at once felt them a thousand fold repaid. I know not whether the recesses of the Hardanger Fjord (which I have not seen) may contain still finer scenery: but nothing that has fallen under my eye in Norway is, in my judgment, at all to be compared with the head of Romsdal's Fjord, and the Valley as far as Romsdal's Horn, for picturesque grandeur, that borders on, if it does not quite attain, the sublime.

I might add, that this is perhaps the only district that fully realized my preconceptions of Norwegian scenery.. The mountains range from 3000 to 5000 feet in height: their sides are for the most part as sheerly perpendicular as it is possible to conceive; while a deep mantle of snow caps their summits, and fills all the ravines, wherever practicable for it to lie. Their forms are withal exceedingly diversified: in the Fjord, they are bold, projecting, massive; but near Romsdal's Horn, they are splintered and peaked into a thousand fantastic shapes. The head of the Fjord branches into two prin-

cipal arms; besides which, there are several
subordinate Glens, of great grandeur, connected with the principal valley. Nor are softer
features altogether wanting to this magnificent
panorama; the Northern shore being much
lower, formed by undulating hills, often well
covered with wood, interspersed with a few picturesque cottages, and patches of cultivation.

The Ferry across from Torvig to Veblungsnæs
is only three miles: but gusts of wind swept down
with such unexampled violence from the Vind
Tinde, (or Windy Peaks, as they are justly
named,) that it was with great difficulty, not
unattended by danger, that we accomplished
the distance in an haur and a half. Here I
found excellent quarters at a " Privileged Mer-
chant's," of the name of Fladmark: and in a
very few minutes forgot all the annoyances of
Ferries, want of sleep, and of food, in the
most glorious slumbers.

Veblungsnæs is a good sized village; and
from its position enjoys a considerable trade

with the interior, as far as Guldbrandsdal. There is a well attended Fair in autumn, frequented by merchants from Trondhjem, Bergen, and even Christiania: but at all other seasons the trade seems to be entirely in the hands of my host, Mr. Fladmark, who is one of that privileged class, which throughout Norway have the sole permission, from the Storthing, of selling the usual articles of consumption, without any other check on extortion, that I am aware of, than their own consciences, and the necessities of the purchasers.

I presume the original cause for establishing these monopolies, was the encouragement of tradesmen to settle in thinly populated districts, by securing them against undue competition. But it must be a bad system: and indeed is attended with so great evils, that Mr. Laing seems to attribute to it chiefly the demoralization of Sweden, of which he gives so frightful a picture; although it equally prevails in Norway, without apparently being followed by

equally calamitous consequences.   However,
I had only to do with Mr. Fladmark in his
capacity of host : and it is but justice to add,
that though his charges were somewhat higher
than those of the country, I found his house,
both in point of accommodations and viands,
one of the very best I met with in Scandinavia.
I staid there three or four days, as well to explore the neighbouring scenery, as to try the
Rauma river, where, I mentioned, two English
friends had very good sport on their way to
the Namsen.

The morning after my arrival, I drove about
six or seven miles up Romsdalen, to a spot
which had been described to me as the best
for Angling. The River there, after struggling
through a long succession of wild rocks, tum-
bles over two or three considerable Falls, which
though not absolutely insurmountable to Salmon, delay many of them in their ascent, and
consequently fill the pools immediately below
with fish. These Fosses are situated at the

very foot of Romsdals-Horn: and though I do
not wish to tire my reader with the reiteration
of my raptures, I cannot omit all mention of
this scenery, which it would be difficult to
parallel for romantic grandeur, in any country.

The lower part of the Valley is broad and
fertile: but the mountains on either side
increase in height as they rapidly converge
above the Foss, so as barely to allow sufficient
space for the road at their rocky base. "The
Horn" itself (as it is significantly designated)
is a most picturesque object, terminating in
two cusps, of which the highest is crowned
by a pillar, to show that even its savage precipices have been scaled by man. Immediately
adjoining it are the shattered peaks of the
Vind Tinde, which rise to very near 5000
feet: and the opposite side of the narrow
gorge is closed by the equally lofty Troll Tinde,
or Witch Cliffs, the most strictly perpendicular,
of any rocks of equal height, that I remember
to have seen. Where all the mountains are

remarkable for their singularly broken outline,
these last are especially conspicuous for their
strange fantastic pinnacles, which, when seen
against the clear blue sky, assume the form
of, and have been named after, owls, dogs,
men, &c.

Olden Tradition says that they are the
Witches and Dæmons of heathenism, transformed into these enduring monuments at the
time St. Olaf christianized this Valley by the
powerful arguments of fire and sword.   I
would not affirm that the modern inhabitants
altogether believe these tales; but I observed
they avoided the subject as much as possible,
and when pressed, spoke "with bated breath,"
and as I thought, with evident respect of these
"Good People."   All mountaineers are super-
stitious; and the Norwegians are by no means
exempt from this weakness, for which some
excuse may be found, not only in the delusive
atmospheric phænomena common to all mountainous countries, and the avalanches of snow

and rock, to which this Valley is peculiarly exposed; but perhaps still more to the almost total seclusion from the rest of the world, in which its inhabitants live.

Before I commenced fishing, I was universally assured that I had come at least six weeks too late: and I soon had reason to believe common report for once to be correct. In the course of several hours that I patiently tried all the best part of the river, for nearly a mile below the Foss, I saw but two or three Salmon rise, in places, where either I could not cast my fly, or the water was too still. The only fish that moved in a favourable spot, I at once hooked, and landed: it proved a pretty Grilse of eight pounds weight. And upon my second visit to the Rauma, two days later, (for rain prevented my returning there the next day,) I rose but one Salmon, in the same pool where I had caught the other, which, however, afforded me better sport, being much larger, and weighing upwards of twenty-one pounds.

Others saw I none : and though the natives
every night netted the larger pools, wherever
practicable, as well as set smaller nets, called
Garns, from the banks (in the same way as
the Kelso fishermen practise during floods in
the Tweed) I heard that they had taken
scarcely any fish for some time. It was therefore evident that such as had not been caught,
had either run higher up, or had returned to
the sea.

The Foss under Romsdals-Horn is sufficiently high and strong to prevent any except
the most powerful fish from ascending in ordinary states of the water : and to increase the
difficulty, " Bygnings," or wooden traps, have
been built out into the most practicable parts
of the Fall, with considerable ingenuity and
success. Higher up, the course of the Rauma
is so rapid and rocky, as not to admit the use
of the Naat, or large net : but Garns, and
traps, are placed at every favourable point, so
as to allow very few fish to ascend as far as

Ormen, where they are effectually stopped by an insurmountable Foss.

These various contrivances for the capture of the poor Salmon have greatly increased within the last few years, and have materially diminished the number of fish within the memory of men now living. All lament the grievous decrease, without being altogether willing to open their eyes to the evident cause. If they will not allow the fish to reach their spawning beds, or spear them with the Lyster, while helpless there, they only resemble the boy that killed his goose which layed him the golden eggs. In a country like Norway, where there are no game laws, no fence months, and where no mercy is shown to a spawning fish, or a bird on her nest, it is obviously the wild character of its mountains and streams alone, that preserves any of their respective tenants from utter extermination. If bounteous Nature did not protect her children, ruthless, avaricious man would soon effect their destruction.

From the middle of June to the end of July is the best season to fish the Rauma. The river, being fed by many Glaciers, will be found of so milkyish a hue as almost to deter an Angler unaccustomed to these Northern streams, from putting his rod together. Salmon will, however, most certainly take a large gaudy fly in snowy water. The same Englishmen before alluded to, killed on an average five or six Salmon a day, on two several visits to this river at the above mentioned season. The greater part were small, in comparison with those of the Namsen; but a few weighed from twenty to thirty pounds. As far as I could learn, they were the only Anglers, except myself, who had ever cast a fly upon this water, except for trout.

The best fishing water is somewhat confined; though enough to afford a few days' amusement during the period that fresh fish are continually running up from the sea. Many parts can be commanded by wading: at others there are a few very indifferent boats; and an honest civil "Huusmand," who lives close by, will be ready to manage them, and point out the most likely spots.

On my return the second day with my largest Salmon, expecting its size would draw forth some encomiums, I found it was quite eclipsed by two magnificent Flounders, that lay on the green before Fladmark's house: they weighed upwards of a hundred weight each, and their captors were vainly endeavouring to sell them for a dollar, or four shillings a piece. I was told they are often taken with the hook, of thrice that size! What a pull they must give! And into what utter insignificance do even Namsen's salmonian monsters sink, in comparison!

The river being in flood from rain that had fallen during the night, I thought it would be a good opportunity to explore the lateral valley of the Ister, a smaller stream that joins the Rauma, about two miles from Veblungsnæs. A

few Salmon ascend it: but it is too still, and too
much encumbered with alder bushes, to afford
good Angling. It was, however, the scenery that
lured me up its banks; and this amply repaid me.

The valley, which is about six or seven miles
long, penetrates into the very heart of the
Bröste Fjeld, whose snowy pinnacles are seen
rising out of extensive Glaciers: the two highest and finest peaks are called the " Sister
Tinde."   Below this region of eternal ice, a
barrier of lofty rocks sweeps down from its
aërial height, with a beautiful steep curve, into
what has evidently been once the basin of a
Lake, and is still in many parts little better than
a marshy jungle, overgrown with the usual
dwarf shrubs of Northern latitudes, and afford-
ing secure refuge to numerous wild fowl.   At
the upper end is a considerable waterfall, fed
by the Glaciers: it makes a good show from a
distance, but when seen nearer, loses some of
its effect from a talus of debris, which receives
its silvery waters, instead of a gulf of rock:

many other cascades, of lesser note, but much beauty, leap over, or glide down, the mural rocks that embrace within their mighty arms the whole length of Isterdalen.

This wild vale was, no long time ago, occupied by several permanent Gaards: they have all been given up, from the uncertainty of the crops' ripening; and it is only now used for summer pasturage. A few starved cottagers yet linger here, whom I could observe peeping stealthily from behind their half-closed doors at the stranger, who was so suspiciously examining their ungenial glen, alone, and as it must seem to them, without rational object.

Early on Thursday, September 5, I quitted my comfortable quarters at Veblungsnæs; and drove to Fladmark, the second stage up Romsdalen, with the intention of ascertaining whether the Salmon that had escaped the persecutions below, were to be met with there. Between Fladmark and Romsdals-Horn, the narrow Valley is filled with enormous blocks, confusedly hurled down from the impending crags; among which the roaring river tears its devious path, as best it can. Therefore, though an odd pool here and there may be found, there can be no continuous Angling : besides which, this wilderness of rock, though magnificent to see, almost defies passage, with rod in hand. Above Fladmark (*i. e.* " The Flat Field,") the course of the river, as might be guessed from the name, is for a long way, much too still.

However, immediately below the Inn, I observed an excellent stream, where, if anywhere, it was evident that Salmon must lie. I therefore tried it twice over, most carefully, from both sides, without seeing the slightest sign of a fish : besides which I learned that none had been taken in the Garn for several previous days. I also fished a pool or two lower down, with the same result; which sufficiently convinced me of the utter uselessness of wasting any more of the few precious days of the waning season, at this river.

Moreover, I had been smitten with a great desire to shoot a Reindeer. On my way from Veblungsnæs, I met a hunter with a couple of these animals that he had shot the preceding week, and which he was taking to the town to sell. And while speaking on this subject at Fladmark, I encountered another Chasseur, on his return to his home near the next Station, Ormen, with the intention of taking the Fjeld early the next morning. After some parley, I agreed to accompany him; and accordingly drove over to Ormen, which he recommended as the best starting place. His name was Lars Larsen paa Stavem: and, as I subsequently discovered, he was obliging, active, trustworthy, well acquainted with the mountains, and possessed of some tolerable notion of the chace; but on the whole, rather more of the Bönder, than the Jäger, of the honest Norwegian Farmer, than the true Chamois-hunter of the Alps.

Had I not already seen the still grander portion of the valley under Romsdals-Horn,

I should perhaps have been more impressed by
the magnificence of this upper part. There is
not a mile of it that does not abound with
beauties of the very highest order. The general
character was a very deep valley, of variable
width, narrow below Fladmark, but considerably wider above; finely hemmed in by mural
precipices on either side, abounding in specimens of rocky scenery, unequalled out of Norway, and beautified with the usual Norwegian
accompaniments of pine forests and waterfalls.
At each turn of the road, were seen, high above
all, the snowy ranges that afforded to these
cascades their never failing supply; and that
looked like the very home and father-land of
the wild deer. These were the general features of the Vale: but the reader will easily understand that there were a thousand details of
grandeur and beauty; and if he have in his composition any of my mountain ardour, he will not
be slow to comprehend the delight I experienced
in contemplating its rude magnificence.

As we approached Ormen, the Valley became more contracted, and the ascent, which had hitherto been comparatively easy, was sensibly steeper. The Rauma here, after rushing through a long rocky gorge, so deep and narrow, as completely to hide its boiling waters, falls at once from a considerable height into a dark chasm. Immediately below which, a scarcely smaller stream, from the opposite mountains, tumbling over the cliffs in several channels, forms so many beautiful cascades, at the point where it joins the main river: it is a grand scene, if not within the grasp of the painter, at least sure to gratify the lover of the picturesque.

I found very indifferent accommodations at Ormen: and to my disappointment, could obtain nothing better than barley bread, cheese, and brandy, (all bad,) either for my dinner that evening, or for my expedition the next day. One needs to have something more substantial, when following the free denizens

of the mountain, over their native Fjelder.
Nevertheless, I rose before daylight the next
morning, feeling equal to any fatigue, and
keenly anxious for the sport.   I was soon joined by Lars; and before five o'clock we started
amid the half suppressed ridicule of the vil-
lagers, at the idea of an Englishman expecting
to shoot a Reindeer.   I thought to myself that
a man who had shot Chamois on the Alps and
the Pyrenees, need not fear the mountains I
saw before me: but aware that it is safer to
boast on one's return than on setting out, I
said nothing.

For the first two hours we encountered a
very laborious ascent up the steep cliffs that
form the lower range.   In one spot we saw
recent traces of a bear: these animals are very
numerous in Romsdalen.   A fine Cock of the
Woods also rose close by us; and throughout
the day we saw coveys of Ryper, as well as
several Alpine hares, at which of course we
did not fire, for fear of alarming the Reindeer.

Upon surmounting this stiff ascent, we reached an elevated plateau, from which snow mountains rose on all sides to a further height of 2000 or 3000 feet. From this point, the walking became easy enough to a mountaineer, and was never dangerous. Lars had no telescope, so indispensable to the Gems-jäger: but unlike them, he was accompanied by a powerful dog, held in a leash; which, if well trained, is not only serviceable in retrieving wounded deer, but also winds them at astonishing distances, and by his movements advertises his master where they are.

We traversed much likely ground, without seeing any thing more than the fresh tracks of three Deer in the snow, which, I suspect, had been disturbed by us, without our observing them. At length, about ten o'clock, we came to a sort of mountain glen, with a few isolated rocks projecting above the surrounding fields of ever-during ice; in short, the very spot for a Chamois, or Reindeer. Here, to my very great delight, I first discovered, with a small pocket telescope, a herd of seven Rein, four old does, and three well grown calves. They were at a considerable distance, but on the move towards us, feeding as they came, and totally unsuspicious of danger.

For a long time, they were so placed as to render it impossible to approach them unperceived : but it was highly interesting to watch them as they cropped the scanty Alpine herbage that bears their name,* or crossed in lengthened file the steep sides of intervening Glaciers, every now and then stopping to listen for sound of fear, or to interrogate the gales if any enemy were at hand. The breeze fortunately blew briskly *from them;* and therefore could tell them nought of us : but our anxiety during all these processes may well be imagined, as two hours elapsed, before they mounted a rock that hid them from our sight.

* Rensblomster.

Leaving then the dog fastened to a stone, we ran across a Glacier, and climbing up a steep precipice as silently and rapidly as we could, crept to the spot where they had disappeared. We were now within 100 yards of them, feeding in perfect security. Lars had a rifle; I had only a double barrelled gun, loaded with ball. In order, therefore, to insure at least one deer, I had previously told him to fire first: but I kept my eye upon him, and his shot was followed instantly by mine. From the position in which I lay, I could only command two full grown calves; but they offered so fair a mark that it was impossible to miss them, and one dropped to my shot: Lars had also wounded another. The remaining five started in wild amaze: and as they bounded across, at about eighty yards' distance, I put my second ball through the leading doe, fracturing both her hind legs, close to the hip.

Three Reindeer thus fell to three barrels, within ten seconds, a feat seldom, if ever be-

fore achieved in these mountains. I must,
however, confess that all three were clumsy
shots, taking effect in the hinder parts of the
animals: so that, though they were completely
crippled, it took us some time to secure them
all, in which we were ably assisted by our four-
footed companion. My poor doe, in particular,
managed to tumble or scramble down a precipice, into a half frozen Lake, where she
continued paddling about, until I sent a ball
through her spine, and the wind soon wafted
her lifeless to shore.

To our very great surprise, we found upon
examination, that one ear was slit, a sure sign
that she had once belonged to the Finns, who
thus mark their domesticated Reindeer. Now
the nearest point to which that singular Noma-
dic race ever come with their herds, even in
summer, is upwards of 200 miles: and Lars
Larsen, who had killed more than 100 deer,
said he had never seen, or heard of, a Rein
with the Lapp's mark upon it. in these moun-

tains before. She had become completely wild
again, to all intents; and from her taking the
lead in their flight, was evidently acknowledged
to be the strongest and most courageous of
the party. We gutted and washed our victims
on the spot; and then placed them under heavy
heaps of stones, to protect them from the various
birds and beasts of prey, that frequent this
chain, such as the Bear and the Wolf, the
Lynx *(Gaupe)* the Wolverine, or Glutton *(Jærv)*
until Lars could return with a horse and friends
to take them home.

The Reindoe, it is well known, is equally
furnished with horns, as the male: but they
were at this season too velvety, and not full-
sized; I, therefore, preferred for my trophy the
three pair of fore legs, which I was proud, on
my return, to display to my sneering friends
at Ormen, and was evidently looked up to with
more respect, in consequence of my success.
The foot of the Reindeer is beautifully adapted
to its mode of life and habitat. It has the same

raised hard edge, that gives the Chamois so
secure a footing on the narrowest ledge of rock;
at the same time it is capable of great dilatation,
to prevent the animal from sinking in the soft
snow, that so commonly forms its path.

We were favoured with such heavenly weather, as enabled us to see the surrounding
snow ranges to the greatest advantage. And
though the eye and heart at once confessed they
were not upon the scale of those with which in
earlier years my passion for Chamois-hunting
made me familiar, yet did I feel and acknowledge in them also, the impress of lonely majesty stamped by the Divine Architect on these
eternal monuments of His Power, which to my
taste, no other earthly work of the All Powerful and All Good can boast.

I felt myself a little stiff, but not much tired,
the next morning, when I started for Lessöe,
on my way into Guldbrandsal. The upper part
of Romsdal exceeds in wildness any thing I had
hitherto seen : the mural precipices that confine

the Valley, with the scanty corn fields in the
centre, entirely disappear, and the road climbs
over a succession of broken, rocky ascents,
many of which might be avoided by better en-
gineering. Hard as these Gneiss rocks are,
however, the river has worn them into chasms
of extraordinary depth, at the bottom of which
its seething waters foam and boil; and whirl
round and round in ceaseless turmoil, until
at length they effect their escape by bounds
and leaps that shake the foundations of the
everlasting hills.

There are innumerable details of savage
magnificence, that might each suffice to confer
interest on a day's excursion; but which, perhaps from their very multitude, can scarcely
be appreciated, or retained, as they deserve.
In many spots I observed some remarkably
aged Scotch Firs, of great girth, and picturesque spread of limb, though not lofty. At a
place called Björneklev, between Brude and
Nystuen, two torrents of nearly equal volume,

the Rauma and the Ulva, form fine cascades, as they descend suddenly from a higher stage of this mountain glen. This is so wild a pass, that the Scotch under Colonel Sinclair, who perished at Kringelen, in 1612, (as before alluded to,) did not dare any longer to follow the road, but are said to have taken to the mountains, and not to have come down again till they reached Eneboe, in Lessöe.

The interest of my drive through Romsdalen was much increased by the traditions connected with this expedition, so celebrated in Norwegian annals. A thousand stories, each surpassing the other in strangeness and improbability are still rife in the valley. Many of them are preserved in a rude ballad, popular among the peasants, which has been poetically paraphrased by the well known Edward Storm. But lest any details should perish of a deed of arms considered so honourable to Norway, my friend the Priest of Vaage, in which Parish Kringelen is situated, has collected them into a little brochure,* which he kindly presented to me.

It seems that during the short war between Denmark and Sweden, that is usually called the War of Calmar, the youthful Gustavus Adolphus raised about 2000 troops in Scotland. The main body, under Munkhaven, after making an ineffectual attempt to surprise Trondhjem, safely reached Sweden, by way of Stordalen. Meanwhile Sinclair's division, variously estimated at from 250 to 800 men, landed in Romsdalen, in July 1612: and having seized a man, named Peder Klognæs, to act as guide, advanced up this savage valley, committing deeds at least as savage, if the Bönder's ballad may be believed. Most of the peasants, however, took the precaution of removing them-

* " Sagn samlede i Guldbransdalen om Slaget ved Kringelen, den 26de August, 1612, og udgivne i Forbindelse med hvad Historien beretter om denne Tildragelse." That is, " Traditions collected in Guldbrandsdal, respecting the Fight at Kringelen, the 26th of August, 1612, and published in connexion with what history relates of this event."

selves and valuables into the mountains, where
as they sat perched on their inaccessible cliffs,
it is said they were assailed by opprobrious epi-
thets and threats, which seem to attest a greater
proficiency in Norsk than one can imagine the
Scotch to have attained.

At some farms they found provisions laid out
for them; and there they usually showed mercy:
but other houses they fired. The narrowness
of the Valley, divided by the impassable chasms
of the Rauma, in many spots afforded opportunity for taking a perfectly safe shot at the in-
vaders: of which the Dalesmen failed not to
take advantage. Amongst others, in this manner they killed two *Turks*, whom veracious tradition affirms Sinclair had brought with him to
hunt out the concealed natives, as they could
infallibly scent out Christian blood, unless their
olfactory nerves were deranged by the smell of
hemp, or of sour milk! Modern interpreters
explain these "wild Turks" to have been
Bloodhounds.

Not, however, to dwell on these traditions, of which each Gaard, and each Pass, retains its stock, the Highlanders reached Guldbrands-dal, where they naturally thought themselves in comparative safety. The military were all absent fighting against the Swedes : but the peasants of the surrounding vallies had collected at Kringelen, below Laurgaard, and prepared an ambuscade, which was so well chosen, that while they lost only half a dozen men,* they destroyed the whole of this disciplined force, except a few whom they shot in cold blood the next day, as "they could not (so says their own ballad) bear the cost so hard," of supporting them, or conveying them to prison. Kragh, however, asserts, that a few did after all escape.

The movements of the concealed Bönder were directed by a peasant girl, named Pillar-

---

* The fight, if such it must be called, took place on 26th August, 1612 ; the monument erected on the spot says, August 24 ; but Priest Kragh shows from better authorities that it was the 26th.

Guri, famed in Döler song, who from a lofty crag which commanded the Pass, gave notice of the Scots' advance, by modulations on her Alpine horn.   The first shot passed through Colonel Sinclair's forehead, killing him dead on the spot: but he is said to have yet had time and strength to exclaim, " That is Berdon of Seielstad's ' shot !"   Without adverting to the curious medical question concerned therewith, it seems difficult to understand how these strangers, who had been but a month in the country were so familiar not only with the language, but with individuals.

I should mention that Sinclair having the reputation of a wizard, Berdon chewed the silver buckle he wore, and therewith formed the bullet that did the deed: lead or iron having no effect on the Highlander's charmed body.   Poor Mrs. Sinclair was also there with an infant in her arms : both were killed, and thrown into the adjoining River Laag; but as she floated down the stream, she is said to have composed and sung, a wild air, which is still preserved. And such things are not only reported among the peasants, but are gravely recorded in print! It is difficult to account for the national enthusiasm respecting this petty episode: Norway has many prouder days to boast, than "the fight by Kriugelen."

To return, however, from this long digression, to Björneklev, at the head of Romsdalen. Upon emerging from this wild pass which so alarmed Sinclair and his stalwart Highlanders, the road runs for some miles through a flat and open valley, that occupies the summit level between Romsdalen and Lessöe. Its elevation is about 2000 feet above the sea: the scenery from henceforward is nevertheless, with few exceptions, very tame in comparison with that already described. The roads are also abominably kept; for which the only excuse that can be made is the paucity and poverty of the inhabitants.

Corn is attempted to be grown here: but it

is evidently beyond the limits permitted by Nature; for this is the fifth successive summer that the crops have been totally destroyed by early frosts. The consequent distress may be faintly imagined: the poorer farmers have already parted with every thing disposable, to purchase a little food, and they have nothing now but starvation staring them in the face. It is a curious fact, that frost is never known in Romsdalen at even higher altitudes than are constantly exposed to it every autumn in Lessöe.

At Nystuen, I met with an adventure that had nearly put a fatal termination to my Tour. A young colt of two years old was there given me for my carriole, which had rarely, if ever, been in any kind of harness before. It was as may be supposed, extremely awkward at starting; but long experience had given me such confidence in these little animals, that I doubted not I should be able to manage it.

However, at the very first descent, directly

that it felt the pressure of the carriole, the half wild creature sprang uncontrollably forwards, like the Reindeer of the previous day; then reared, and struck out with his fore-legs, snorting and shaking his head: and finally, just as I jumped out, fairly leaped over the slight fence on the lower side of the road, a sheer fall of at least ten or twelve feet, whence horse and carriole bounded three or four times over, down a steep precipice towards the River; until they were fortunately stopped by some stumps and bushes.

At the very moment that the frantic animal sprang over the fence, I had the long reins so entangled about my legs that I thought I must inevitably be dragged down with it. I scarcely know how I escaped: I can just remember throwing myself on my back, and shuffling the reins off as well as I could: but never shall I forget the sentiment of thankfulness to Him who has so often preserved me during a very adventurous life, which thrilled my breast, as I saw my vehicle somerseting down this frightful place. Every thing, I felt convinced, must be broken to pieces : but how little did that matter, in comparison with the merciful preservation I had experienced !

However when we came to examine, we found one shaft broken in two or three places; but this, with a few minor fractures and scratches, was the sum total of damage. Three bottles that were in a case attached to the splash-board, were not even cracked: and yet the equipage had tumbled forty or fifty feet, and performed at least three complete somersets ! The cause of the disaster, too, stood confined by the harness to the stump of a tree, as quiet as a lamb, and trembling violently from head to foot; but without the slightest injury of any kind ! It seemed incredible.

With some difficulty we got the light little carriage up into the road; and while my servant was engaged in temporarily repairing the damage, I returned to Nystuen, and entered a temperate complaint in the best Norsk I could command; for which, I doubt not, the Farmer would be fined, as he amply deserved to be, for supplying so unfit a beast. When I consider the variety of horses I drove in Norway, and the perilous roads I traversed, it is wonderful that I have not more dangerous accidents to record.

The scenery was seldom calculated to withdraw my meditations from my late escape: the vale was open, flat, and boggy: the hills comparatively low, and sweeping tamely down into it: those looking to the North were clothed with undisturbed pine forests; those with a Southern aspect were diversified with a few scattered Gaards. The summit of this mountain plain is occupied by a considerable Lake, which offers the singularity (not unparalleled in Norway) of a copious stream flowing constantly from both ends, which are of course at exactly the same level.

Close by its Eastern termination are exten-

sive buildings, the remains of some iron works,
which were given up some twenty years ago, in
consequence of the failure of fuel.   At this
season, large trout ascend the streams of the
old works, from the Lake of Lessöe, for the
purpose of spawning; and are killed with the
Lyster as much as twelve pounds in weight.
There seemed to be a tolerable Inn; where I
could have been content to stay a day or two,
for the purpose of trying whether the fish
would take the fly here, but my arrangements
did not permit me to do so.   Near the next
station, Holseth, at the head of Lessöe Lake,
great numbers of fine trout and grayling are
also caught in the autumn; and at another
stream, a little to the Southward, named
Laardal's Elv, still more and larger fish are
said to be taken: the Inn at Holseth seemed
to be indifferent.   The next day being the
Sabbath, prevented my giving these rivers a
trial: I doubt not they would amply reward
the Angler that will try them at this season,

when the trout leave the deeper waters of the Lakes.

From Holseth I drove along the Northern shores of Lessöe Vand to Holager, where I took up my quarters. The contrast between the two shores of this Lake is great, the Southern side is rocky, steep, and left nearly in a state of nature : while that through which I had passed, slopes more gradually towards the water, and consists of a deep, stiff clay, covered with corn fields and Gaards. They have a custom here, which I have only elsewhere remarked in Dovre Præstegjeld, of placing the sheaves of corn to dry against double rows of hurdles, called Shĕgārs, instead of the usual upright poles described by Laing. This is accounted for by the very high winds that harry through this transverse Valley from the Dovre Fjeld to the Western Ocean.

I had a pretty good sample of the violence of these winds. On Sunday, September 8, it blew a perfect hurricane, accompanied by driv-

ing rain, so as to detain me within doors; and
when I sallied forth the next morning, it had
not much moderated. However, in spite of a
blustering east wind, I embarked with my
landlord on the Lake; and fished down to
its termination, about an English mile. I
caught on my way four trout of three-quarters
of a pound each; but it was evident that most
of them had retired into the streams. Earlier
in the season, I am confident from all I saw and
heard, that this Lake must afford excellent
trout-fishing.

I then tried the stream that issues from the
Lake: and here, to my surprise, I not only
found several boys angling with worm, but one
man fly-fishing. He had picked up a little of
the art from some Englishmen; his tackle and
performances were alike rude: however he
failed not to spoil one or two of the best places.
I fished down for about a couple of miles. I
met with a succession of beautiful streams; and
besides a vast number of small trout and gray-

ling, rose several of two and three pounds.
I caught three of the former, and one of the
latter weight; and on a shallow some way down
killed a fine trout of seven pounds, which for
some short time fought and struggled like a
Salmon.

I saw enough to convince me, that in right
weather and season, capital sport may be had
here; and, perhaps, still better at the head of
the Lake. There are also many Lakes at various
distances in the mountains, containing large
and well flavoured trout: and the landlord of
Holager has a portable boat on purpose for
such expeditions.

In the first stage Southward the next day,
I crossed a good stream, issuing from the
Siouge Vand, as pure as crystal, between two
regular walls of sandstone rock : it is celebrated
for its trout, but the lower part at least seemed
too *torrenty* for the Angler. I then joined the
road over the Dovre Fjeld, a little above Lien ;
and thus again entered Guldbrandsdal, which

appeared doubly soft and beautiful after the
sterner features of the scenery, with which I
had so long been conversant. The reach of the
river Laugen, from Lien to Tofte, is, both from
character and appearance, by far the best
adapted for fly-fishing of any part of that river;
below Tofte it becomes too broad and still; and
lower down, near Sell, the waters from the
Otte Vand, always turbid from the melting
Glaciers, completely discolour it for many
miles, so as to put any attempt with the fly out
of the question.

I will not, however, dwell upon any more piscatory details, which I would rather reserve for
a separate Chapter. I passed with delight un-
diminished along the lovely Eastern shore of
Lake Mjösen: and for the second time entered
Christiania from Raaholt, in the same abomin-
able weather, so common at this season. I
mention the weather, because it both times
rendered the road as nearly impassable as can
be conceived. For nearly forty miles it was one

eternal wade through unfathomable sludge, where I was only assured of the fact of there being any bottom at all, by bumping against the huge stones therein engulfed. All the roads round Christiania are disgraceful to the vicinity of a capital; but this surpasses them all: it is difficult to say whether the strength of the poor beasts, or the philosophy of the driver, be the most severely taxed.

CHAPTER X.

General description of the Scandinavian Lakes and Rivers—
Salmon Rivers of Norway: The Alten; the Guul; and
minor Rivers; the Siva; Ranma; Bergen Streams; the
Mandal, &c.—Laaven, near Laurvig—Falkenberg—Rivers
on the Bothnian Gulf—Trout Streams of Norway; of
Sweden—Flies and Tackle—Advice to Anglers.

In addition to the scattered notices dispersed
throughout these pages, it may, perhaps, be
acceptable to the Angler, if I here give a general description of the piscatory capabilities of
Scandinavia. Not that I pretend to be acquainted with each of its thousand Rivers, and
ten thousand Lakes; but at any rate I can,
either from my own experience, or from trustworthy information, give some account of the
principal streams, that will prove useful to the
stranger, and which at least I know I should

have been thankful to obtain, when I first came into the country. I will take care to record nothing, except from personal knowledge, or from authority that may be depended upon.

The number and size of the Norwegian Rivers strikes an Englishman at first as extra-ordinary for the extent of the country. This impression may partly arise from the roads being necessarily carried along the banks of the largest streams and lakes; but there can be no doubt that they are much more numerous than in a flatter and more Southern Land. Norway consists entirely of mountains, covered for the most part with deep snow, which during the hot, though brief Summer, pours down inexhaustible supplies of water into the Vallies. The spongy nature of the lower mountains, and the inequalities of the surface, sufficiently ex-plain the abundance of Lakes.

The rocks, over which the Rivers run, be-long to the hardest, subcrystalline, primary family: and the fall is usually very great. It is, therefore, to be expected that their course should be extremely rapid, often tumultuous; and that they should frequently be crossed by barriers, forming what in Norsk are called Fosses. This same rocky character of their beds renders the rivers of Norway less suited for trout, than for Salmon. There are no worms, or larvæ, or insects brought down by each flood to feed the former: while Salmon seeking little or no food, in the fresh waters, which they frequent only for the purposes of continuing their race, delight in the pure coolness of these pellucid streams.

Accordingly, there are scarcely any Norwegian rivers of proper size that Salmon do not enter. And they would, doubtless, be all even better supplied than they are with this noble fish, if it were not for the Fosses which too many of the largest rivers have near their mouths, and which prevent the Salmon from ascending, on their annual passage from the sea, to their spawning beds. This is most lamentably the case with the Glommen, the Götha, the Drammen, and the Skeen Rivers: in fact with all of any consequence that empty themselves into the Fjord of Christiania, except the Laurvig river. When it is seen on the Map what an enormous proportion of the drainage of Eastern Norway, and Western Sweden enters the sea by these magnificent channels, it will be understood what a grievous loss to the Angler it is, that those splendid Falls of Trollhættan, Sarpfoss, and Högsund, are not further removed from the mouths of their respective rivers. All the many streams that feed the vast Wenern, the Mjösen, the Randsfjord, and others, are thereby deprived of their noblest inhabitant.

To begin with the Northernmost point. The establishment of a steamboat at Trondhjem, which sails every fortnight to Hammerfest, has rendered a voyage to the Arctic Circle comparatively easy: therefore the Angler who may be tempted to admire the sun at midnight, or to stand on the North Cape, will not be sorry to learn that there is a good Salmon river, at Alten, a little to the South of Hammerfest. I know from Englishmen who have tried it, that large fish are occasionally caught there: at the same time, as an English company has long been established at Alten for the purpose of working the neighbouring mines, I presume the river is pretty well fished. However, from all the accounts I have received, the society of these gentlemen will amply compensate for any inconvenience of their rivalry.

I am not aware that any of the rivers between the Alten and Namsen have ever been fished with fly: though there can be little doubt they all, more or less, contain Salmon. Of the Namsen itself, and the neighbouring streams, the reader will think that I have already said enough. The Bangsund river is frequented by a fair number of Salmon and sea trout; but it is not well adapted for An-

gling, even if any one could be induced to
delay at a third rate stream, when so near to
the King of Salmon waters. I have recorded
my opinion of the Steenkjær, and other rivers,
that fall into the Trondhjem Fjord.

In addition to the hints before given, I need
only further mention, that in consequence
of Mr. Laing's description, I was induced
to make an excursion for two or three days
into Værdal, where he had a Farm, close below
a Foss that stops the Salmon from ascending
higher. I rose but three small Grilse; and
though a few fish may occasionally be caught,
I am satisfied that great sport can never be
had here: netting is extensively practised.
The Valley itself however is well worth visiting,
and the Gaard where I lodged, Östgrund, was
particularly comfortable. At a very picturesque
Fall, about three miles higher up the Valley,
I hooked several fine trout: and if I had been
better prepared for trolling, I ought to have
had much greater success.

The Nid, under Leerfoss, whatever it may have been formerly, I do not now consider worth fishing, unless for the sake of enjoying the beauty of the scenery, and the converse of the intelligent proprietor.

By far the best river in the North of Norway, next to the Namsen, is the Guul; which one Englishman, who fished it for several summers, and was well qualified to judge, even preferred to its great Northern rival. It is much smaller, so as to be in general commandable with a long rod by wading: the fish also are not so large, a thirty pound Salmon, being at least as rare as one of forty pounds in the Namsen. I have merely tried it *en passant*, never under very favourable auspices, and only near Rogstad. But the gentleman alluded to staid on its banks more than one season for six weeks; and is universally said to have had excellent sport.

My lists will show what I did, in indifferent weather: I can at least attest that it is a remarkably pretty Angling River, and that the

Valley is one of the most pleasingly picturesque I ever saw. Rogstad is the best quarter: but on my way to Röraas, I observed for many miles higher up a beautiful succession of streams and tempting pools: which so pleased my eye that if at any time I were driven off from the Namsen by the superabundance of rivals, it is undoubtedly on the banks of the Guul that I should take refuge.

Of the Örke and Suren I have said sufficient in the last Chapter, to give the Angler an idea of their qualities. On the Totals Elv (at the head of the same Fjord into which the Suren flows) there is a Foss, near its mouth, which prevents any Salmon from entering it. But at Hævi, somewhat further to the North, are two rivers frequented by Salmon; in which, I was assured by a native of the place (whom to my surprise I found bargaining for artificial flies in Trondhjem) that two Finns caught many large fish a year ago, with very rude tackle. Hævi lying not far from one of the roads to

Hitteren, it is just possible that a sportsman in pursuit of the Red deer, for which that island is so famous, might take these rivers on his way, and be glad to learn what chance of sport they afford.

The next river, as we advance Southwards, is the Driva. A few Salmon, I know, ascend it, as far even as Drivstuen; but the greater number are stopped by weirs near Lönset: I cannot speak from experience, whether lower down there be good Angling, but should imagine it to be at least as good a stream as the Rauma.

Of the Siva River, which falls into the Lange Fjord, opposite to Eidsvog, I heard so tempting a description from a sergeant who resides there, that nothing but invincible obstacles prevented me from giving it a trial. He informed me that there is no Foss to hinder the Salmon from ascending to the very sources of this mountain stream, which in its course passes through three considerable Lakes, full of large trout, grayling, and Char. He also said there are pike here: but if he be correct as to the character of the fish, it is the only instance I am aware of, in these parts, of the existence of that tyrant among the finny tribe. No Angler has ever cast a line here: the Salmon are caught in considerable numbers by a sort of weir; which however is not allowed to cross the entire stream.

Next follows the Rauma, for the character of which I need only refer to the last Chapter. Besides the Ister, which I have also there mentioned, there is a small stream at the extremity of the Fjord, near Heinden, frequented by Salmon: however, my two English friends, before mentioned, not only killed no fish in it, but met with a very unpleasant reception from the natives, who seem to have misunderstood their object.

The only Rivers that I have personally examined along the Western coast, South of Romsdalen, are those at Skjolden and Leirdalsörén. But I have seen and heard enough of the others to give a tolerably correct general idea of their capabilities. From the conformation of the Norwegian Continent, (the mountains rapidly increasing in elevation as they approach the Western sea,) the rivers on that coast are all comparatively short in their course, and their waters remain in a more or less turbid state, until the very end of summer; that is, until the snows that feed them, have entirely disappeared, or the sun has no longer power to thaw them. Good Salmon fishing cannot therefore be expected: though I have heard of some being caught in one or two of the Bergen rivers, and at Fretton; and doubtless a few fish might be killed there, sufficient to interest a Tourist who explores that most magnificent district for its scenery, but far from enough to tempt any one thither merely for the Angling.

It is very possible there may be some tolerable Salmon rivers, between Stavanger and

Mandal, as the mountains recede from the coast: I can only say I never heard of such. Sir Humphrey Davy has spoken of the Rivers at Mandal, Christiansand, and Arendal; in all of which he saw Salmon rise, but never caught any, being there for a very short time and in unfavourable weather. He, however, caught a great many sea trout, which he says abound in the Southern streams, whereas they are far from being plentiful in the North. The Mandal is usually considered the best of these rivers, though somewhat spoiled by saw-mills. At Skeen, there is unfortunately a Foss that hinders Salmon from ascending its fine and copious stream.

But incomparably the best Salmon river in these parts, and perhaps the second in all Scandinavia, is that near Laurvig, the Laaven, the same that passes by Kongsberg. It is not many years since its full merits were ascertained: but several Englishmen who have lately tried that part of it near Staberöd (where

the great Southern road crosses it) which
abounds with favourable rapids, have had excellent sport. I fear that at all these Southern
rivers, the Angler will not only meet with more
rivals among his own countrymen, but also
more impediments from the natives, than on
those of the extreme North, where I have
chiefly fished.

I have already alluded to there being no
good Salmon rivers on either side of the Fjord
of Christiania: I may add that, with the
trifling exception of the stream at Jonserud,
above Göthaborg, there are none along the
whole Western coast of Sweden, until we come
to Falkenberg. Sir H. Davy also fished this
river, and had what he considered a good day's
sport, (" Salmonia," page 142,) but others
have had much better. The principal feeders
of Falkenbergs An flow out of low hills, from
which the snow early disappears; so that it
is usually in order by the latter end of April.
I know a gentleman who during the whole

month of May, last year, averaged upwards of
fifty pounds in weight each day, previously to
the young Grilse making their appearance in
the river. From his list, the fish seemed rarely
at that season to be under seven pounds, still
more rarely above twenty pounds. The worst
is, that the Angling water is very confined,
extending little more than a quarter of a mile;
in which there is one good pool worth all
the rest. A staked and bound weir allows
scarcely any fish to pass: and those caught
by the Angler must be surrendered to the proprietor, or paid for, *more Scotico.*

Salmon are taken at Halmstad and Laholm:
indeed Copenhagen is chiefly supplied from
those rivers: but I do not believe they are
suited to Angling. The Southern portion of
Sweden, Scania, &c. contains no streams
wherein any fish better than an eel, or pike,
will live.

All the Swedish rivers, however, which
empty themselves into the Bothnian Gulf,

contain abundance of Salmon. It has been estimated that from Tornea to Stockholm, there are at least fifty considerable rivers, many of them exceedingly large, every one of which is frequented by Salmon. Unfortunately, the Western shore of the Bothnian Gulf is so flat for a long distance inland, that the universal character of these streams is too sluggish, too deep, too muddy, for the fly fisher; offering, in short, as great a contrast as can be imagined to the gigantic torrents of Norway, and much rather resembling the Götha above Göthaborg.

Vast quantities of fish are taken in nets by the natives; and I cannot doubt that they may be killed with the fly, by a competent Angler, who will pursue any suitable river up to the hills where its earlier course is spent, and where it must form the rapid streams and roomy pools that delight the Salmon fisher. This at least I know, that in two or three instances, where a very inadequate trial was made, with very insufficient means, the success was enough to prove that good sport might be had with better means and appliances to boot. I much wish that some really accomplished Angler would try a few of the best rivers of Northern Sweden: and by choosing his points well, where the hills come near to the coast, and by arming himself with proper information, I have every confidence he would enjoy a most capital summer's fishing, in waters almost unknown to Anglers.

Having never visited that district, I do not like to risk misleading my reader as to the most favourable spots, by mentioning my crude ideas: but I can at least assure him from trustworthy information that he will find the Angermann River, a little to the North of Hernösand, well worthy his attention; especially from Hullsta to Hämra, near which latter place is an extensive Sawing establishment, from whose proprietors I am much mistaken if he will not meet with every possible assistance and attention.

The Salmon of these rivers are said to be extraordinarily well fed, short, and fat: which is attributed to their feeding on a particular kind of small fish abundant in the brackish waters of this landlocked Gulf. Grayling also abound, as likewise fine perch in certain rivers: and in all the mountain Lakes are magnificent Char, which take the fly well, wherever a tolerably sharp stream enters. The accommodations, however, and living, become detestable even for Scandinavia, immediately that the traveller quits the great roads.

Having cast this brief *coup d'œil* over the Salmon Rivers of Scandinavia, let us return for a moment to Norway, and give a few general hints as to what the trout fisher may expect there. It would be useless, even if I were capable of it, to particularize one half of the Rivers and Lakes of this well watered country, all of which, as far as my experience extends, contain trout more or less plentifully. Yet I scarcely know how to point out the best places where first-rate trout fishing may be insured. The truth is, that Salmon being my chief object, I have never gone out of my way, or devoted much time, in pursuit of trout. The summer is so brief, and the distances so great, that it is impossible for one ambitious of fishing the Northern rivers to waste many of the precious days of the fleeting season, in exploring unknown streams.

I have accordingly fished only such Lakes and Rivers as came in my way, which either from information or appearance promised to afford sport; and I tried few for more than an hour or two: my list will show with what success. My sport was frequently good, considering the adverse circumstances under which I fished; but it was scarcely enough to repay an Angler who should come from England mainly for trout fishing. Such an one, however, would, I doubt not, in any part of Norway, very soon surpass my performances, if he gave himself a little trouble to acquire information, and to resort to the most favourable points.

It shall be my object now to give such hints
as I think likely to be generally useful. The
first enemy to the Angler in Norway is snow-
water : I have learned by experience that Salmon will take the fly in rivers discoloured by
melting snow; but not so trout. The higher
mountains of central Norway should, therefore,
be avoided until summer be far advanced: and
even among the hills of the South, the streams
are rarely in tolerable order until the middle of
May; more frequently it is Midsummer before
any good sport can be expected.

Large rivers are also objectionable : they
seldom contain so plentiful a supply of trout
as smaller streams, except at certain Rapids, or
Fosses : while but a small portion of them can
be commanded with the rod. By far the best
for the Angler are moderately sized streams,
that pass through Lakes of similar dimensions :
the fish fatten and attain great weight in the
still water, and at favourable times come into
the streams to feed and enjoy the fresher ele-

ment. It is this very character that makes the chain of Lakes near Jerkin so good, where though I have never taken fish above three pounds, I have seen them spring of double that size.

The heaviest trout will invariably be found lying at the foot of Falls, especially if the Fall is situated a little above an extensive Lake; as in the case of Hundfoss between Lillehammer and Moshuus. Numbers of large trout collect there in the Autumn, and are taken occasionally up to thirty pounds in weight, in a kind of trap. The body of water is so vast and tumultuous, as not to afford any Angling to my taste, but a gentleman of my acquaintance killed here on one afternoon of September, two trout of fifteen pounds each, with the fly. I feel quite certain that both here, and at other similar Fosses, the troll would answer far better for these monsters, than the fly: but not liking that mode of Angling (killing, as it confessedly is, for large fish) I have seldom tried it.

I cannot say that I observed any marked peculiarity in the flies adapted to the Norwegian Waters; except that perhaps the palmers did not answer so well, as the winged flies. I usually found the best Scotch Lake flies the most successful: a well made Scotch "Professor," if of the right size, will kill anywhere.

The whole of the extreme South of Norway abounds with good Angling lakes and streams: as for instance, the neighbourhood of Christiansand, and Arendal. The district of Tellemarken, round the Gousta Fjeld, has long been celebrated not only for the exquisite picturesqueness of its scenery, but for the excellence and abundance of its trout. An English Angler, of the name of Hutchinson, long resident in Drammen, has this year (1839) published a little Treatise on Fly-fishing, for the express use of the natives.* He seems to speak

* " Fluefiskeriets Anvendelse i Norge:" i. e. The practice of Fly-fishing in Norway ; by Robert D. Hutchinson, Drammen, 1839. It is accompanied by well executed plates, explanatory

of Wigersund, near Modum, and Lake Sperild (through which the Beina flows in its course from Valders) as two of the best waters for trout in that neighbourhood. But he must be by far the best qualified of any one, to give accurate information as to the piscatory capabilities of this portion of Norway; and which, I doubt not, he would be happy to communicate to any brother Angler, who should properly apply to him.

The Beina, as well as all the Valders waters, were too chilled with snow water, when I passed by them at Midsummer, to be fit for Angling: later in the season, I doubt not, they afford good sport. The Hurdal Vand, near Raaholt, has the character of holding many and fine trout. The Mjösen Lake is too full of pike; and none of the lateral streams that

of every thing used either in fly-fishing, or trolling; as also of artificial flies, in every stage of their manufacture. No doubt this little work will contribute to render an art peculiarly English much more familiar to so good imitators, as are the Norwegians, with such opportunities for its exercise.

fall into it are good. Of the Laag, Loug, or
Lösne (for it bears all these names) that chiefly
feeds it, I have already spoken: if the water
be in order, a fair number of trout may be
killed in it, near Laurgaard; from Lie to Tofte,
however, is a still better reach.

The Otte Vand, on which Lomb and Vaage
are situated, is totally unfit for Angling: but a
little to the South of it, in a Valley named
Hedal, I was assured upon competent authority that there is an abundance of trout and
char. And if the Sportsman be adventurous
enough to pursue this wild valley some thirty
miles, up to the Sætters at its head, he will
find a chain of small Lakes, called Finster Aa
Vand, below the great Bygdin Vand; which
at least contain large and well flavoured trout,
for I have eaten them, from three to five
pounds in weight, with flesh of a deeper red
than Salmon. I am only afraid that from
these Lakes being situated near the highest
range in Norway (the Jotun Fjeld) they may

possibly be too discoloured for fly fishing, until late in the Autumn.

There are also numerous Reindeer in the neighbouring mountains; and not being much disturbed, they are more easily approached than in more frequented districts. It must, therefore, be a capital quarter for a Sportsman, who is well prepared to rough it, there being no permanent residents. The Landlord at Moe (from whom I chiefly obtained this information, corroborated by friends at Vaage) possesses Sætters, or Chalets for the Summer pasturage, at the very head of the Glen, and will be most happy to render every assistance in his power to the bold Adventurer. I much regret that I did not explore it; the scenery at any rate must be magnificent.

I have already said enough in the last Chapter to give the reader to understand what excellent sport may be had, at the proper season, in Lessöe Lake, and the streams that flow into, and out of it. Also the Lakes of Jerkin have

been sufficiently described: the early part of
the Driva (before it descends into the Valley
of Kongsvold) is full of small trout, of which
an unlimited quantity may be taken in favourable weather.　　　　　　　　　-

While at Röraas in 1837, in the course of an
unsuccessful expedition into the mountains on
the frontiers of Sweden, for the purpose of
seeing an encampment of Lapps, I fished the
extensive Lake Öresund, as well as one of its
principal feeders, at a Fall near Brække, where
at that season (September) there ought to have
been large trout. I rose, however, but one
good sized fish; and caught a few small ones.
I had better sport on my way back to Röraas,
in the stream that issues out of Hitter Söe:
and still better, on a subsequent day, in the
more copious river by which Lake Öresund discharges its waters. Very heavy fish frequent
the latter, which is well suited for fly-fishing,
still more so for trolling. I was not lucky in
the day; the heaviest trout I landed weighed
three pounds, but I rose better fish, and saw

still larger jump in the water. This stream is the young Glommen : in the lower part of its course this splendid River nowhere appeared adapted to Angling; besides, it is too much infested with Pike.

Sælboe Söe, near Trondhjem, is reported by good Anglers to be one of the best Lakes in Norway : the trout are large, and usually take the fly freely. I have not tried it: but from personal experience I can guarantee any tolerable Angler to fill a very large basket in a very short time, at the Lake of Hammer, on the way to Steenkjær; if he be but moderately favoured by weather. When I have been at Hammer, there was never wind enough for the larger fish to take the fly; although I saw many of great size spring in the water : but during the few hours I angled there, on three several occasions, I rose trout from half a pound to a pound, nearly as fast as I could cast my fly. There are also ducks and other aquatic birds to be shot, in the Autumn.

I will conclude this imperfect catalogue of

the principal trout-waters in Norway that lie on the Tourist's road, by again referring to the Værdal River, where at the Upper Foss (about three miles from Östgrunden, see page 117) fine trout may be taken by the troll, for which it is a favourable spot: and by penetrating still higher up the Valley, towards Sweden, numerous lakes are met with, universally described as full of large trout, that take the fly greedily.

Having alluded to the Salmon Rivers of Sweden, I will add a brief notice of the few in that kingdom where I have taken trout. The Angling reader will recollect that upon my first visit to Trollhættan at the end of May 1837, I killed a few very fine trout below those magnificent Falls. One weighed ten pounds and a half, the heaviest trout I ever took with the fly: others were of five and four pounds each. They at the time appeared to me identical with the Salmo ferox, of the larger Lakes in Scotland: and specimens of the same having been since submitted to Mr. Yarrell, by Mr. Lloyd, that eminent Ichthyologist has pronounced them to be such. There can be no doubt that they come down from Lake Wenern, the second largest body of fresh water in Europe; and not being able to return, harbour in the quietest holes they can find by the side of that rushing world of waters.

Below the Foss at Lille Edet, on the same River, trout of great size, as well as Salmon, are also taken: it is scarcely a place for the fly, but the troll might perhaps answer. Bleak, for bait, are easily procurable at Trollhættan. A short way above the Falls, I have caught well-sized trout at certain spots, where a few islets cause a trifling current: but by far the best point is at Öna-foss, six or seven miles higher up the Götha. Mr. Lloyd, the well-known Author of the "Northern Field Sports," has established a fishery there; and, I understand, in some summers has taken as much as six thousand pounds' weight of trout. Those that are not caught in nets, he chiefly kills with the troll; not caring to use the fly for such monsters, which occasionally exceed thirty pounds, and frequently twenty pounds. The Game Laws in Sweden being infinitely severer than in Norway, he is enabled to keep off poachers in some degree: but I fear it has cost him considerable annoyance and trouble.

Lake Wenern itself not only contains these gigantic trout, but also pike, chub, burbot, &c.: and in my judgment is not at all adapted to Angling: neither are any of its Southern tributaries, with which I am acquainted. On its Northern and Western coasts, however, (for it is quite an inland Sea) from Åmal to Carlstad, are many Lakes and streams, said to afford excellent Angling. At Dejefors, on the Klara, fourteen miles above Carlstad, great quantities of trout are annually taken below the Fall. The Klara is the principal feeder of Lake Wenern; it is of great length, collecting all the drainage, and bringing timber down from the very neighbourhood of Röraas.

. The water that issues from Lake Wettern is far clearer than that of the Wenern. Indeed it is so pure, as even in the middle of the Lake to taste like spring-water: and as the very few streams that feed it, are strikingly incommensurate with the body of water that flows out at Motala, it is the universal opinion that it must be chiefly supplied by subaqueous springs.

The latter end of May, the trout seem to leave the crystal depths of Lake Wettern, where they had taken refuge during the winter, and appear on the streams at Motala. They are killed there of great size, with the Lyster, the worm, and even a rude troll: also here and there in wooden traps. In consequence of the number of mills and other obstructions at this point, I preferred accompanying the Steamboat to Husbyfjöl, a small village, near the exit of this same River from a lower and much smaller Lake, called Boren. Here I staid a couple of days: and though I

caught only sixteen trout, they weighed thirty
pounds. The weather was bright, and yet very
cold; unfavourable enough for fly fishing.

I found also on the spot a native Angler who
plied the fish, early and late, with worm and
bait. His tackle was very uncouth, but by
perseverance he killed several fine fish: and
still more interfered with my sport, by being
on the water before me. He paid some trifle
to the Landlord of the Inn for liberty to
angle: and though I was armed with the
same permission, he did not half like seeing
me pull out so many fine fish, which he had
been vainly endeavouring to catch. The largest that I landed weighed upwards of four
pounds: besides four others of three pounds
each.

I know not where I have seen so many large
trout as here; and it is very possible that there
may be infinitely better places than I was
able to discover during the afternoon and
morning that I spent there. An English

gentleman, some time resident in Stockholm, came to this river for several summers; and is reported to have had great sport. The Angling would be infinitely better, if there were not too well constructed weirs, about a mile below Husbyfjöl: they by no means catch all the trout, but they much injure the river, and annoy the Angler.

I fear I can hardly add any thing useful to the hints I have already given on the subject of flies and tackle. Patterns of those I used may be seen at Martin Kelly's, or at Evatt's : and if I were again to go to the Namsen, I should take most of the same kinds. Any hook smaller than that commonly used for the strongest treble gut Irish flies, is nearly useless : single gut, such as we employ for summer fishing in Scotland and Ireland, is quite out of the question in Norway. I do not dislike those patterns of Tweed flies, that resemble a long, rough hairy worm; but for the Namsen, I should prefer having them retied on Irish hooks, with the addition of a rather handsomer wing.

For the Guul, and such other rivers where constant casting is required, smaller Salmon flies must be used; but still I recommend them to be of good size, and invariably on treble gut. An English Gentleman, who fished on the Namsen in 1838, killed many of his heaviest Salmon by trolling with a small fish. I have no doubt that in certain states of the water, this may be a successful method; but, I confess, I like only to take my fish fairly with the fly, and rarely will employ any other mode, even for trout. Perhaps even the "red berry," or prepared Salmon roe, might prove as killing here, as it undoubtedly has been found elsewhere. But I look upon this method as but one degree removed above worm fishing, and but two degrees above netting; and totally unworthy of any fair Angler, who fishes for sport, not for the pot.

I consider a well oiled silk line as preferable

in fishing the Namsen, because it runs better
off the wheel, and takes up less compass than
a patent line: but for casting I prefer the
latter. The Angler ought to be provided
with each, of not less length than 100 yards;
120 yards are still better : I have several times
had 150 yards run out in a few seconds, while
I was rowing to the shore : but it is the far
wiser plan to follow the fish with the boat (as
I have before · described) in these first desperate plunges, which are usually down the
stream : since, with that length of heavy line
out in the Rapids of the Namsen, it is almost
certain to be entangled round a rock.

The Salmon fisher should further have one
stout rod, twenty feet long; and a second,
somewhat lighter, but of nearly equal length :
together with a two handed trout rod, of
sixteen feet. He will, of course, get them
of his own maker: but I doubt if he will find
any more to be depended on for quality and
strength, than those manufactured by Eaton,

in Crooked-lane. They should all be provided
with a spare third joint, and two or three tops
to splice: ferruled tops for Salmon rods I
especially eschew. Each of these rods must
be fitted with a strong leather case, which
Eaton knows well how to make; and they can
then be safely strapped under the shafts of
the carriole, if the traveller's equipage admits
of no better place.

And these general directions, I think, are
enough for the purpose I have in view: for I
pretend not to write for the Tyro, who needs
to be reminded of the minuter articles of his
craft that he must bring with him, or who
requires instruction as to how he is to cast
his fly, or manage his fish when hooked. Such
beginners have no business on the Namsen;
they must commence with more pastoral
streams.

My only advice is, to let the fly sink moderately under the water, and to take care that it
invariably swim up and down the stream, not

awkwardly across it. Next, to keep the line perfectly *taught*, by which means the Salmon will hook himself, with very little assistance from the Angler. When hooked, if he be a large fish, handle him firmly, though somewhat gently at first; but as soon as his first violence is foiled, and he is half coaxed, half drawn, into the safest spot that lies near, then bear upon him boldly, as much as your tackle will well sustain.

By handling a heavy Salmon too roughly, at the moment he first feels the hook and is in possession of his full strength, you run great risk of angering him into desperate plunges, that, if the hold be indifferent, or the place dangerous, may effect his escape. However, on no account suffer a fish ever to get the line loose: for one Salmon that escapes by being held too tight, fifty are lost by the looseness of the line permitting the hook to fall out. Of course, when a large Salmon exhibits a determination to rush away, line must be given him:

but let him not have a yard, that he does not
fight for; and the instant that you feel him
begin to turn, draw him in, and shorten line;
prepared to repeat this process, until his
strength be fairly exhausted, and he is content
to float near enough to the shore to be gaffed—
an anxious moment, especially with an awkward Norwegian attendant, so different from
the accomplished gaffers of the Tweed, or the
Shannon.

Not only steadiness of hand and eye is required in controlling the energies of an active
Salmon; but also considerable presence of
mind, as often, when a fish is making for a
dangerous point it must be decided in a single
instant how and where he is to be turned; or
whether it be most advisable to run the risk of
breaking the tackle, by forcibly withholding
any more line, rather than suffer him to reach
his point.

The reader also, who has perused my
sketches of Angling on the Namsen, may

perhaps have collected that the nerves are occasionally tried by perils, not to the tackle, or the poor Salmon, but to the Angler himself, at least on the upper part of that noble, but wild stream. How much does this risk and difficulty enhance the glorious sport, while the enthusiast fondly fancies it almost dignifies it!

But I dare not indulge myself any further on a theme that must appear incomprehensible rhapsody to any one not smitten with the same passion; for a passion it is, if it be felt at all, and circumstances admit of its developement: while the true Salmon fisher will acknowledge the same sentiments in his own breast, and only complain that I have expressed them so inadequately,

CHAPTER XI.

A TRUCE now to piscatorial details. But before quitting a country, through which I have wandered with so much delight, I would wish to add my mite of information respecting its general geological features. Geology has of late years become so popular a science among all ranks, that it is to be expected many whom sport or the picturesque may chiefly lure to this romantic land, will also cast a scientific eye on its rocks : for, whatever may have been the case in Dr. Johnson's time, Anglers are proud to know that, in our day at least, the foremost philosophers and artists do not disdain the gentle craft : the hammer often accompanies the fishing rod.

Besides, the geological structure of Norway too much influences the character both of the rivers and the scenery, not to be interesting to every tourist. To the former it gives their numerous Fosses, their rapidity, their purity, when not contaminated by Glaciers : to the latter, its sheer walls of rock, its splintered cliffs, its longwinding Fjords, which form so characteristic a feature of the savage grandeur of Norway. By far the largest portion of the surface of Norway is occupied by those ancient rocks (formerly called Primitive, or Primary,) from Gneiss, through an infinity of varieties, down to Clay slate; and which in all the countries where they appear, are at any rate the oldest, the loftiest, and the hardest, that come under our observation.

I should suppose that there is not in the world so favourable a field for studying this most intricate and important Group of rocks, as here. With the exception of the "Transition Territorium" of Christiania, and a comparatively small tract in the extreme North, they extend over the whole of Norway : while from various circumstances connected with their mineralogical character, and the violent upheavings they have suffered since their original deposition, they frequently present to the geologist perpendicular faces of hundreds and even thousands of feet, where he may observe upon a gigantic scale, not only the contortions of strata, but the interesting changes of mineralogical structure.

On the other hand, there are many difficulties in the way of the geologist, who would trace out the relations of these rocks to each other, and reduce the probable mode and sequence of their origin to any thing like order. There is an enormous extent of wild mountains, each presenting peculiarities which require to be studied, in order to obtain a complete idea of the history of these obscure formations. Then the summer, during which alone the higher ranges can be traversed, is lamentably brief: and the travelling becomes very difficult, directly the main roads are quitted; indeed, to one unacquainted with the language, or unprepared to rough it as to living and accommodations, it may be described as almost impracticable. None, therefore, but a native can be reasonably expected to furnish a complete geological Map of this country.

At the same time, I feel strongly convinced that this department of Science would be infinitely benefited by even a single summer's visit of any of our first English Geologists, really qualified for this task; and particularly of him, who is universally regarded as our great authority on the subject of our own older

Rocks. If he would only examine carefully the most instructive localities that lie convenient for observation, near the principal roads, I doubt not that his acknowledged powers of penetration and classification, would throw most valuable light on these puzzling formations, and afford a clue to unravel many of the seeming mysteries of their origin and relations.

I am not aware that any English geologist of eminence has visited Norway, except Mr. Lyell, who did not, I believe, extend his observations beyond the territory of transition and plutonic rocks, 'with which he was more interested. I am equally unacquainted with any first rate French geologist, who has ventured into the interior of Norway. Professor Naumann, of Jena, has published in German, some account of several "Wanderings" through the most interesting mountain districts;* which is

* "Beyträge zur Kenntniss Norwegens, gesammelt auf Wanderungen während der Sommer-monate der Jahre 1821 und 1822. Von Carl Friedrich Naumann. Leipzig, 1824."

extremely valuable as furnishing details of many important localities, difficult of access. But independently of his having viewed this land nearly twenty years ago, which in a science that has advanced so rapidly as Geology, is a momentous consideration; Professor Naumann rather gives an accurate statement of isolated facts, than a comprehensive view of the relations of extensive groups, or any enlarged theory of their general history. Von Buch's still earlier Travels remain, perhaps, even at the present day, the most valuable contribution, by any foreigner, to Norwegian Geology.

Norway possesses only one native Geologist of note, B. M. Keilhau, Professor of Mineralogy and Geology, at the University of Christiania. He is a man of undoubted intelligence and possessed of great knowledge of his science, both practical and theoretical. He has devoted many summers to the close examination of the Scandinavian rocks, from the Western Fjords to the confines of Sweden, from Lindesnæs to

the North Cape, and even to Spitzbergen.
He has communicated great part of the results
of his investigations in a Norwegian periodical,
entitled "Nyt Magazin for Naturvidenska-
berne:" and the rest will doubtless follow, in a
language unfortunately little accessible to the
generality of scientific men. Professor Keilhau has likewise lately published in German, a
full description of the "Transition Territory"
of Christiania, together with a coloured Map;
which must be looked upon as a most valuable
contribution to the Geology of his native
country.

The Professor's views upon many Geological
subjects, especially with regard to what have
been termed the Metamorphic Rocks, are very
peculiar; which renders it the more desirable
that the phænomena on which his views are
founded, should be submitted to the examination of competent Geologists, not wedded to the
same opinions: preconceived theories too often
involuntarily bias the judgment of the most

impartial observers.   Keilhau, himself, is most
anxious that his facts and deductions should be
subjected to the rigorous criticism of his scientific brethren.   He is convinced that they will
eventually be found to bear out his theories.
At any rate it seems certain that nowhere can
the relations of what are now commonly called
Plutonic rocks (though Keilhau does not admit
the appropriateness of the name, as involving a
theory of their igneous origin) to metamorphic
rocks, be more extensively or more usefully
studied than in this district.   Whatever may be
thought of the Professor's theories, there can
be no doubt that Norwegian Geology is deeply
indebted to him, not only for the description
and map of the Transition district already alluded to, but also for a most laborious and important collection of facts, embracing nearly
the whole of the kingdom.

Gneiss is allowed to be the most abundant
formation in Norway.   But in speaking of it,
or the other primary rocks here developed,

considerable latitude must be allowed : mica is
often wanting, so also is felspar : and very
often, hornblende is either associated with
these two ingredients of Gneiss, or entirely
replaces them. A composition of hornblende
and quartz is common in the North : and in
some spots, as on Rundene, on Sneehættan, in
Gjendal, &c., the rock seems entirely composed
of quartz, which splits into very thin laminæ. I
observed no slate rocks like our own, with true
slaty cleavage : but silicious rocks that admit
of extensive and even separation in the plane
of their stratification, (similar to the flagstones
of our coal formation,) are found in many
parts, and occasionally are used for roofing.

Every variety of rock, belonging to the families of Gneiss, pure and syenitic, hornblende
slate, mica slate, quartz rock, chlorite, and
clay slate, down to the most friable shales,
may be seen ; and very often appear to run
into each other, in a manner very puzzling to
a tyro. Then there are numerous rocks called

by the older Geologists, such as Esmark and
Naumann, Grauwacké: under what title we
should now class them, I know not; they have
the mineralogical character belonging to that
proscribed family. Indeed, the difficulty of
accurately distinguishing many of the Norwegian rocks by names recognized in other countries, is so great, that excellent Geologists
differ considerably in their nomenclature of
the same formations.

The lines of stratification are not always
strongly marked : though it may invariably be
distinguished, with more or less difficulty, that
the rock really is stratified. Speaking generally, the Norwegian Rocks are not much
contorted, neither do they dip at such high
angles, as might be anticipated, in the case
of formations of so great antiquity; since the
deposition of which the Globe has suffered so
many violent convulsions.

As being probably connected with this comparative absence of disturbance, it may be

mentioned, that there is scarcely any trace of
granite or other Plutonic rocks, within the extensive Primary district. This is a remarkable
fact, when taken in connexion with the enormous developement of igneous rocks, within the
Transition territory; but, I presume, must be
explained by their having burst through the
incumbent mass of least resistance.   There
is a small granitic district, on the Eastern
coast of Finmark, not far from the North
Cape : but nowhere in Norway, except near
Christiania, have I seen veins of granite (common in the Gneiss of Sweden) or greenstone,
or trap, or other intrusive rock, so frequent
among the older rocks of Scotland.   The
Serpentine mentioned by Esmark as occurring
near Röraas, must be quoted as a rare instance
of a rock, now generally considered to be of
igneous origin, within the Primary district.

Occasionally fragments of an older Gneiss
are found imbedded in regular strata of the
same rock. I have observed other instances ;

but the best examples with which I am acquainted are at Rostan, above Laurgaard, and at the Ferry of Heel, twenty miles to the North-east of Trondhjem. Near the latter place, there are evidences of considerable disturbance, in the contortions of the adjoining strata: the fragments are large, irregularly disposed, a little rounded, and completely amalgamated with the mass, so as to have the appearance of being fused into it. At Rostan, the imbedded fragments are smaller, more conformably arranged, as if squeezed within the layers of the Gneiss; their edges, as Esmark says, are for the most part sharp, but the felspar is rounded. I looked in vain for any extraordinary signs of ancient convulsion in this vicinity.

Hard as these primary rocks are, there is not a mountain valley that does not afford evidence of their surfaces having been extensively worn down, in the course of long geological periods. The depth of detritus which

is observed in Værdal, Orkedal, or near Trondhjem, for instance, is enough to astonish one,
if we regard the excessive hardness of the
rocks, from which it is undoubtedly derived.
In the first locality, especially, it is not a deposit of large fragments torn from their parent
cliff, and a little rounded by attrition; but an
enormous thickness of fine silt, interspersed
with small gravel; which seems to attest, not
one or two great convulsions, but long continued wasting and rolling processes. The
destructive processes, to which the Norwegian
rocks are exposed, are commensurate with
their durability. That great agent for trans-
posing the constituent parts of our Globe,
Water, exerts its energies on a gigantic scale.
Without speaking of the larger rivers that
roll through their vallies, with an impetuosity
that nothing seems capable of resisting, there
are unnumbered torrents, fed by the perennial
snows, which hurry down the fragments of the
higher mountains, that have been loosened by

frost and rain; and after breaking and pounding them in their headlong course, deposit the fractured and rounded masses, with the associated silt, in a yearly increasing talus, which may be invariably observed at the first level point these streams reach, from the upper ranges.

The effect of this power of transportation is greatly increased by the vicissitudes of temperature, to which Norway is peculiarly liable. Its brief summers are intensely hot; its long winters proportionably severe: hence the water, which during the former season percolates every fissure and crevice, becomes frozen to the lowest depths it has penetrated, and by its expansive power rends asunder its rocky prison.

Norway is doubtless indebted to these atmospheric agencies for much of its romantic grandeur, its shattered crags, and perpendicular precipices : while to the seemingly destructive, yet really beneficial element, that brings portions of the hard mountains from the regions of eter-

nal frost, in a comminuted form, into the vallies
below, it owes all the cultivated land in its interior.   This mass of detritus, on which the
Norwegian Gaards are almost without exception situated, is most commonly disposed in
successive tiers of terraces, rising one above the
other, with great regularity.   Three such tiers
appear to be a very usual number in the north :
I have seen them rising from fifty to one hundred feet above each other.   No one, I conceive, can examine them without coming to the
conclusion that their conformation is owing to
the action of water, which must have stood at
those respective levels during considerable periods, to allow of such vast accumulations.

    In confined Vallies, removed from the sea, I
doubt not these terraces are frequently connected with the bursting of natural barriers, that
had previously kept the water at a higher level;
indeed, there is not a Foss that does not supply
evidence of being now lower in height, and
further up the stream, than it formerly was.

But in the case of broad Vallies, opening wide upon the sea (as in the Fjord of Trondhjem) and where the hills that enclose them, recede, as they approach the mouth, without there being any appearance of barrier across them, it seems to me difficult to account for the quantity of gravel, &c., that occupies their entire breadth, except upon the supposition of an elevation of the land within the period that the mountains and rivers assumed their present conditions.

The Valley of the Nid, near Trondhjem (as well as Stordal and Værdal on the same Fjord) is of considerable width, and is covered with terraces of rolled gravel, not only much above the present level of the river, but even of high water mark. If it had ever formed a Lake, there would be some traces of the rocks that had retained it at a higher level. As this is not the case, we must suppose that it was formerly at a comparatively lower level; when it would form a bay, into which the river would bring detritus, to be there rolled and arranged, in the way common to quiet arms of the sea.

Accordingly, shells similar to those now found in the neighbouring Ocean, have been discovered at various spots round this Fjord, (now raised considerably above its present level) particularly the whole way from Steenkjær to the Snaasen Vand. Two intelligent Scotchmen, located there as Farmers, told me they scarcely ever dug to any depth in the adjoining Vallies, without finding beds of shells, some whole, some broken, just as they would lie on the shore. They estimated the greatest height at which they had observed these deposits, to be 100 feet above the sea. But this is nothing in comparison with the evidences collected by Keilhau, who has discovered *balani* adhering to rocks, many miles inland, at a measured elevation of 470 feet above the sea: besides observing deposits, which he has strong collateral reasons for believing to be marine, at a height of 600 feet.

Keilhau has been induced by the interest which of late years has been attached to the question of the elevation of Scandinavia, to make a personal examination of almost the entire coast, from Christiania to North Cape, with the express view of determining this question, as far as possible, with regard to Norway. He has given a full account of his researches and conclusions, in a late number of the New Magazine of Natural History, published by the Physiographical Society at Christiania, in 1837. His qualifications for the task, and his industry in accomplishing it, seem to leave little for his successors to add upon this point.

He has accumulated a great mass of evidence, both from Man and his earliest works, and from still more ancient records of Nature. He every where questioned the oldest fishermen, as to any observed or recorded alteration of level, in their neighbourhood; and he specifies all the monuments erected by the earliest inhabitants upon the coast or islands, together with their present height above the sea: besides which, he hunted out every trace of marine deposits, of which he could obtain any information. From all these he comes to the conclusion, that they afford no positive proof of any elevation of any part whatever of Norway, within the period of History : but that from the concurrent testimony of seafaring men in the South of Norway (for towards the North this testimony diminishes) in reference to " the sinking of the sea," as they express it ; and also from the position of some works of the aborigines on the South and South-west coasts, it is a " probability not altogether to be rejected," that the Southern portion of this country, may have been a little elevated, since it was first inhabited. This is rendered the more probable by the fact of its being the nearest portion to Sweden, which has undoubtedly been elevated within the historical period.

The amount of this rise would seem from one

remarkable monument of the olden time (the "Snekkestöer of Spangereid") to be about ten feet: whereas certain monumental stones (similar to our Cromlechs) upon very low islands between Arendal and Christiansand (as likewise others in Bukke Sound, and elsewhere) prove that it cannot have been any thing like so much, at that point at least, since they were erected. We must therefore either suppose that the elevation occurred subsequently to the erection of the first mentioned, but prior to the last; or else, that it has not been constant and universal throughout the district. Indeed, if we are at all to receive the evidence of fishermen as to the rise of rocks within their memory, we must at once reject the idea of any such constancy and universality; since a gradual rise of less than one foot in fifty years would not be observable in each man's life: and this would amount to twenty feet in 1000 years, an elevation, which, it can be proved to demonstration, has not occurred at many places within the last ten centuries.

The Professor next shows the impossibility of any appreciable change of level in the northern part of Scandinavia, since it was inhabited by man, from the position of many ancient monuments, to which he refers; such as those on the island of Atle, and on the point of Agdenæs. In Nordland and Finmark the idea of a "sinking of the ocean" seems to be much less generally entertained.

But allowing that the evidence preponderates against the supposition of any observable change of relative level between the sea and the Norwegian continent, since the latter was inhabited by men who have left records of their existence, it is at any rate certain that what may be called the monuments of Nature prove very clearly a considerable elevation of the land, up to a period so recent, that all Geologists would assign it to the very latest division of the Tertiary Æra, or even to the commencement of the existing order of things. Keilhau has discovered shells, belonging to the same species as now inhabit the Scandinavian seas, at a height of 470 feet on the South-east coast of Norway; which prove that a change of level must have occurred to that extent at least : while he has traced beds to a further height of 150 feet, which have every appearance of a marine origin, though they do not contain fossils.

Ancient coast lines may also be observed, not only in the soft loose soil, but even in the mountain ranges of hard rock, high above the present level of the sea: also Volcanic Scoriæ, and other foreign substances, are found in various places, either as isolated blocks, or in deposits of gravel, evidently due to the action of water. The shells are seen at every elevation, from the extreme height above mentioned, down to the present shores ; and at certain places form vast banks. These facts attest long periods of disturbance, succeeded by equally long periods of rest. The shells belong to animals that do not live in deep water: and the banks, just now spoken of, are necessarily litoral, and require considerable time for their accumulation: while, certainly, the impression on the rocky cliffs could not be effected except by the long continued action of the waves.

Whether this elevation of the land was slow and gradual, or due to violent and isolated movements, the Professor does not think there is evidence to decide: but he seems to incline to the former supposition. The South-eastern portion of Norway, and a part of the Province of Trondhjem, afford the most undeniable proofs of a geologically recent elevation of the coast to a great extent: but if we allow the erratic blocks and similar phænomena to be connected with the same cause, we are carried back to a period when not merely the lower hills of the Northern continent lay beneath the ocean, but even the loftiest mountain ranges scarcely emerged from the surrounding waters.

Limited beds of crystalline limestone, more or less pure, are interspersed among the primary rocks of Norway, in a manner very common to that family: near Steenkjær the Scotch farmers before mentioned have burned this lime with success for agricultural purposes. The mica slate on the Lake of Sælboe, near Trondhjem is thickly studded with small garnets; and is used for grinding-stones. A kind of Steatite is found near Lomb and Vaage, on the Lake Otte Vand, and is employed for stoves and other domestic purposes, to which its property of resisting fire adapts it. Chrome also exists in the same neighbourhood; as also near Röraas, and in many other localities: and there doubtless are innumerable other mineral treasures, yet undiscovered, throughout the impenetrable district of the Norwegian Fjelder.

The richest mine of copper within Norway, is at Röraas, near the junction of the great Dovre and Kjölen ranges. It is situated in chloritic slate; but Serpentine, both common and noble, according to Esmark, composes several of the adjoining mountains : and masses of crystalline limestone are found lying detached on the surface, in sufficient quantities to supply what is required for the flux of the metal. The smelting-houses are in the centre of the little town of Röraas : they are not distinguished by any novelty or ingenuity of the processes employed, or by grandeur of scale, when considered as the principal of their kind in the kingdom. The ore is first baked in large heaps, to get rid of the sulphur, with which it is almost invariably combined : it seems in general rich, although little native copper is obtained here.

Röraas is remarkable as being one of the only three or four inland towns that Norway can boast. It is entirely supported by its mines : and lying, as it does, 2100 feet above the sea, not only higher than any kind of corn will grow, but even beyond the limits of any of the fir tribe, every thing is necessarily very dear. The mines are situated at a further height of nearly 3000 feet; making a total altitude exceeding that of Jerkin on the Dovre Fjeld. I examined the mine nearest to the town, which is called " Old, or Storwarts Grube :" it is six or seven miles from Röraas.

The usual law, that where there are subterranean treasures the surface should be sterile, is certainly not departed from here: it is barren and ugly. But on the day I visited the mines, the air was so clear, pure, and bracing, as to be highly exhilarating; and the views of the Dovre Fjeld, and my old friend Rundene with its many beautiful peaks, were alone sufficient to reward me for the excursion. Storwarts Grube is situated on the summit of an undulating heathy hill: they tell the usual legend of its discovery having been made by a Reindeer scratching up the moss that concealed it, just as a man was on the point of shooting; and the event is commemorated by a picture in the church.

The vein comes to the surface, and dips at an angle of about forty degrees to the north. They have worked down it, in an irregular manner, about 1000 feet; leaving masses of ore at proper distances to support the roof, and pursuing the vein wherever it promised to be most profitable. The works consequently branch into various passages, which are sometimes low and narrow, but oftener wide and lofty, so as to resemble rude halls of ample dimensions: when lighted up with the flambeaux of a numerous retinue they have a picturesquely solemn effect. This effect is occasionally heightened by blasting the rock with gunpowder, which in these confined caverns produces a tremendous explosion, that causes the tympanum of the ear to vibrate so long and so much, as, I should think, might easily cause or cure deafness.

There are three shafts to draw up the ore and the water, by means of water wheels about thirty feet in diameter: how lamentably inferior to the engines of the Cornish mines! The ore is generally rich : such of it as is too poor to be smelted at once, is pounded and washed in the ordinary way. About 150 persons are employed at this mine; besides which there are several others in the neighbourhood; and at Dragaas, near the head of the river Guul, on the road to Trondhjem, are also large copper smelting works. At this last place may be seen a remarkable conglomerate, containing huge angular fragments of quartz; and likewise a celebrated circular basin in the rock, called "the Witches' Cauldron."

The silver mines of Kongsberg, being so near to Christiania, have been too often visited and described to require much notice from me. They afford an argentiferous lead ore, irregularly disseminated through a hard, compact, quartzose rock, belonging to Gneiss : and occasionally, very large masses of native or pure silver occur. The mine belongs to Government, and supplies employment to nearly 200 men: its produce has been very variable in former years, but latterly has much improved.

A magnificent Adit, of considerable width and height, has been driven, to the distance of an English mile, directly into the solid rock. It is boarded so as to afford easy walking; and terminates in an ample chamber, whence perpendicular shafts descend to a depth of about 1600 feet. The descent is far from being so easy as that of Röraas: it is effected by successive stages of ladders; and by no means repays the fatigue of attempting it. I should, however, strongly advise the tourist to penetrate to the end of the Adit, which, considering its dimensions and the hardness of the rock, surpasses any tunnel I have seen: while the chamber into which the ore is drawn up, filled, as it was when I saw it, with uncouth swarthy figures, and lighted with numerous fires and flambeaux, seemed to me a worthy Hall of Vulcan, so deep within the bowels of the Earth.

Arendal, and other places in the South-eastern district of Norway, afford the chief supply of iron: but it is far less abundant here, than in the sister kingdom of Sweden. The metals obey here the law so generally observed elsewhere, of being developed much the most frequently and abundantly, near the lines of contact of Plutonic with sedimentary rocks.*

However, the district most generally interesting to Geologists is probably that which has been named by Keilhau "the Transition Territory of Christiania." It forms a basin of an irregularly triangular shape, bounded by two walls of Primary Rock, which meet to a point about the centre of Lake Mjösen, and thence gradually diverge in a South-westerly direction, the one constituting the Eastern shore of the Mjösen, and the Fjord of Christiania; the other occupying the Western bank of the Lakes Rands and Tyri, and thence running by Kongsberg and Skien, &c., to the Lange Sunds Fjord, where it meets the Sea.

* Gæa Norvegica, p. 125.

The whole of the intermediate space is occupied
by argillaceous, calcareous, and arenaceous
deposits, intermixed with extensive tracts of
granite and porphyry.

The numerous fossils contained in these deposits prove that they belong to the ancient
group of rocks, lately named and admirably
described by Mr. Murchison, as Silurian. But
it remains still to be shown whether the order
of succession observed in South Wales, obtains
equally in the Norwegian beds. Professor
Keilhau as yet doubts whether such order can
be made out : but it is hoped that ere long, the
Author of the Silurian System will himself
visit this interesting locality, and decide the
question by an examination of the rocks and
their contents on the spot.

That very singular crustacean of the Fossil
World, the Trilobite, is exceedingly abundant
in the neighbourhood of Christiania. The rock
is so hard, that perfect specimens are not easily
procured : and the history of this extinct ani-

mal is so very obscure, as to render it difficult accurately to distinguish its various species. Above fifty varieties, however, have been discovered in Norway; and to a certain extent described by Lector Boeck : they are all strictly three-lobed; there is none that resembles Murchison's *Bumastus*. *Trilobites expansus*, and *Tr. crassicauda*, are by much the most abundant ; *Tr. extensus* (as well as a few others) is supposed to be peculiar to Christiania.

Of the Family *Terebratula,* there are at least twenty-five species, many of which are new. Among them I may mention *Terebratula Wilsoni* (Sowerby) *Ter. plicatella, Atrypa aspera, Atr. lenticularis, Atr. reticularis,* (with the variety named *alata,* by Hisinger) also *Atr. retrusa,* new. The pretty little *Delthyris cardiosperma* (or *ungula*) is found here, but not abundantly : *Leptæna depressa* is more common: as also *Lept. rugosa, Orthis zonata,* &c.

Gypidia lævis (Goldfuss) is not uncommon : there are many species of *Orbicula,* and *Tur-*

ritella : with five or six species of *Orthoceratites ;*
but this last Cephalopod is neither so numerous
nor so large here as in Sweden. A considerable number of a supposed species of *Lituite*
have been discovered lately in forming the
approach to the new Royal Palace: as also a
few specimens of *Conularia quadrisulcata.*

In some spots, that very obscure fossil, which
has been variously named *Graptolithus, Prio-
don, Prionotus, Fucoides Serra,* &c., is found
in great quantities; often much pyritized. It
was long doubted whether it belonged to the
Vegetable, or Animal Kingdom : and though
Professors Nilsson and Beck are most probably
correct in classing it with the Family of "Sea
Pens," still its position in the scale of being
must be considered as not yet fixed. In
Christiania an idea seems to obtain that it was
somehow or other connected with the Trilobite,
or Orthoceratite, in the way of an antenna, or
something analogous : they have, however,
never been found in connexion.

Some of the islands in the Fjord of Christiania are so composed of fossil corals, as to present quite the appearance of a coral reef: the finest specimens come from the island of Langöe, near Holmstrand. Among them are an abundance of *Calamopora*, (*Gotlandica*, &c.) (*Favosites of Murchison*) *Cyathophyllum*, (*vermiculare*, &c.) *Catenipora escaroides*, &c. Columnar joints of *Crinoidea* are found in the island of Malmöe, and elsewhere: but I saw no good or perfect specimen of Encrinite.

In the above catalogue, I have of course only mentioned those fossils which appeared to me the most interesting, either from their abundance or characteristic peculiarities. A bookbinder, of the name of Lösch, usually has a few specimens for sale on moderate terms; and will accompany the Geologist to the best localities. There is a pretty good collection of Norwegian Fossils in the Museum belonging to the University; as well as a still completer series of rocks to illustrate Professor

Keilhau's peculiar views respecting the passage of different rocks into each other.

Perhaps a more favourable spot for examining the changes produced in the sedimentary rocks by those which are now almost universally allowed to be of igneous origin, cannot be found, than here in the Transition territory of Christiania. By looking at Keilhau's map, it will be seen that isolated tracts of granite, syenite, eurite, and porphyry, occupy large spaces, more or less surrounded by slates, limestones, and sandstones of various characters. It is observable that throughout this district (without exception, according to Keilhau) granite is always associated with clay slate, porphyry with sandstone, and eurite with alum slate; from which (corroborated by other reasons) he is led to imagine that by some chemical agency, which he expects the future progress of that science will elucidate, perfectly differing substances may in the course of time have been so completely changed into each other, that clay slate has been converted into granite, sandstone into porphyry, &c., by this mere agency, without the addition of heat, or the introduction of any substance from without.

Keilhau further advances against the Huttonian theory, that granite, when it comes in contact with gneiss, so gradually and insensibly blends with it, as often to render it impossible to say, where one begins, or the other terminates. This fact seems to be confirmed by Mr. Lyell, in his paper read before the British Association in 1837; and it is the more remarkable, when we consider the immense time that must have intervened between the formation of these rocks, according to all the usually received theories. The transition rocks *rest unconformably upon* the gneiss, which must therefore have been both deposited, and disturbed, before their deposition: while granite is in many places seen to cut through all the fossiliferous strata, and must consequently be younger.

Wherever granite thus cuts through the transition rocks, it invariably alters them to a greater or less extent, sometimes for but a foot or two, in one instance for nearly an English mile. This difference of visible effect is an argument urged against the Plutonists by Keilhau; but it is surely not only easy to suppose, but necessary for the explanation of many other phænomena, that the molten masses, of which granite consisted, were protruded at very different degrees of temperature, without taking into consideration the differing conditions, for conducting heat, of the rocks into which it was injected. It is, however, observable that though the effect of the intrusive granite is so great, that soft argillaceous beds are transformed into hard compact slate, and dark, lenticular limestone into crystalline marble (as at Gjellebeck) yet the dip and strike of the sedimentary strata remain alike unaltered.

Extensive veins of Eurite porphyry, and

of greenstone occur in the stratified beds near Christiania; the character of which they always more or less alter, but never interfere with their strike or dip. The former usually lie as a sort of conformable bed between the layers of limestone and clay; and are wider and more irregular in their shape than the greenstone. The greenstone veins are narrow, and perfectly regular in their sides; and cut through both the eurite and the fossiliferous strata, nearly at right angles to their strike, or in a direction about N. N. W., and S. S. E. They have not however disturbed the line of stratification, so that the differently coloured seams of the argillo-calcareous beds may be seen in a perfectly correct line on each side of the interposing dike.

In giving the former veins the name of Eurite porphyry, Keilhau would wish to be under-stood as applying it to the whole class, which must be considered together in a geological point of view, notwithstanding they vary somewhat in mineralogical composition. Quartz is frequently so predominant in them, as to render them by no means easily fusible; though usually felspar is sufficiently predominant to justify the name. It appeared to me that the eurite occasionally spreads out over the surface, (as for instance, at Pipervig, near Christiania,) while the greenstone, from its superior hardness, stands out like a wall high above the softer transition rocks.

It would seem from the phænomena now mentioned, that after the deposition of the calcareous beds, cavities were formed between the strata, into which the eurite was gently injected: and that subsequently, transverse fissures were effected, in the same masses (whether by desiccation, or by contraction of the earth's crust to accommodate itself to a globe diminishing in volume as it cooled) in a direction perhaps determined by electricity, which were eventually occupied by greenstone, protruded from beneath.

In witnessing the immense extent of derivative rocks of the oldest age, which occupy the whole length and breadth of Norway, with the comparatively trifling exceptions already mentioned, one cannot help speculating, whence were they derived ?   It surely is far from satisfactory to say that such enormous masses have been derived from the abrasion of previously existing rocks, of which confessedly no trace now remains : for no -one, I believe, in any country pretends to · show existing granite older than gneiss.   Time we give *ad libitum :* but what a vast granitic continent must have existed, to supply by its waste the enormous extent and thickness of the Scandinavian Fjelder ! what huge rivers, to convey the wasted particles and fragments, and deposit them over so wide an area !

But even granting all this, these vast original mountain chains must have been both more extensive, and loftier, than the sediment derived from them (which constitutes our mo-

dern loftiest ranges) how then can they have so
entirely disappeared from the surface, in any
conceivable disturbance to which this Globe
has been subjected? they would surely have at
least an equal chance of surviving any cata-
strophe, as the inferior strata, formed at their
feet from the abrasion of their surface.

The ingenious hypothesis that much of the
gneiss, though derived from granite, may in
fact be said to be contemporaneous in formation
with it, serves to remove some of the difficulty,
but not all. According to this idea, granitic
matter being protruded into warm, and slightly
agitated water, such as probably constituted the
primæval Ocean, there crystallized into granite, which was partly abraded, almost simultaneously, and deposited in the form of gneiss.
The apparent passage of these two rocks into
each other, in the environs of Christiania, may
be thus explained: but I confess that upon this,
as upon a thousand other points connected with
the fascinating science of Geology, very much

appears to me to remain yet to be cleared up; if ever it can be.

I will conclude with repeating my hope that it will not be long ere this interesting and instructive district be visited by English Geologists, capable of decyphering and elucidating the rich, though obscure records it contains, of the earlier processes, by which the Almighty Architect was pleased to bring our Globe into its present state of order and beauty.

I cannot pretend to have made by any means a complete Tour of Sweden; but having visited some of the most interesting geological localities, in the centre, the West, and the extreme South of that Kingdom, I will add a brief sketch of them, the rather as they lie little out of the direct road to the country I have more especially taken upon me to describe. A good Geological Map* of this portion of Sweden

* Geognostisk Karta öfver Medlersta och Södra Delarne af Sverige, af W. Hisinger. Stockholm. 1834. (Geological map of the Central and Southern portions of Sweden.)

has been published at Stockholm by Hisinger; which the Geologist will do well to purchase : it is not dear, but is difficult to procure, except at Stockholm itself.

Generally speaking, the country from Christiania to Helsingborg consists of Gneiss. But near Wenersborg (at the South-western extremity of Lake Wenern) also at Kinnekulle, near Lidköping, on the same Lake; and again to the South, from Sköfde to Falköping, are some very remarkable protrusions of Trap, surrounded by fossiliferous strata similar to the transition rocks near Christiania.

The extensive district here alluded to, lying between the vast Lakes Wenern and Wettern, is extremely flat. Its base is Gneiss, horizontally stratified, and covered for the most part with a marshy, peaty soil, intermixed with boulders and gravel. It has evidently been under water at no very remote geological period; and would be so again, were the gorge at Trollhættan blocked up a few feet above its present level.

The singular features of this district are well seen from the summit of any of the isolated trap rocks above mentioned, particularly from Kinnekulle: but the effect of closing the outlet of the immense body of waters collected in Lake Wenern (as it doubtless formerly was closed before the rocks at Trollhættan were riven asunder) is best seen from Hunneberg or Halleberg, near Wenersborg.

These are two twin hills, with long, straight tops, from 300 to 500 feet in height, and composed of a kind of trap, resting on stratified limestone. They are now separated by a deep and narrow gorge, through which it is believed the waters of the Lake once flowed : but they have every appearance of having once been united. The Southern side of Hunneberg (which alone I had time to examine) presents a steep escarpment of trap rock, in some places rudely columnar. Beneath the trap lie the calcareous beds, bearing evidence of having been considerably altered by heat, but perfectly

horizontal and undisturbed in their stratification; and seemingly extending some way into
the hill under the trap. I suppose, therefore,
that the latter must have been poured through
a comparatively small fissure, in a very fluid
state, and have then overflowed the limestone
beds on all sides.

The limestone is quarried for agricultural
and domestic purposes: in the two quarries
that I visited, I could observe that it frequently
seemed to be calcined, was vesicular, and contained pyrites, and clusters of crystals, together
with some curious depressed, spherical concre-
tions. The only organic remains, that I saw,
were a few imperfect *Trilobites*, and an abundance of that most singular little Crustacean,
now extinct, the eyeless *Battus*.

But Kinnekulle is a still more interesting
point, both for the Geologist and picturesque
Tourist. Although its height is only 900 feet
above the sea; it yet from its insulated position, on the very shore of Lake Wenern, com-

mands a very extensive and pleasing prospect over land and water. The borders of the Lake are too low to boast of grandeur; but many promontories that run far into its placid bosom, being well wooded, and occasionally occupied by noblemen's seats, afford an agreeable resting place to the eye. On a very clear day, I could but just distinguish the opposite shore in one or two points.

On approaching Kinnekulle from the nearest town, Lidköping, you come first to a platform of Sandstone, resting on the universal Gneiss of this country. It is about seventy feet in thickness, and contains few or no distinguishable fossils. Above this is a second platform, of Alum slate, fifty feet thick, also surrounding the central nucleus, but of course with a diminished diameter: numerous *Battus*, and imperfect *Trilobites*, and crystals of alum are found in this bed. We ascend next to a third platform of reddish limestone, full of *Orthoceratites* of immense size, though not of

many varieties : it is said to be 165 feet in
thickness. And lastly, above all these Transition beds, rises the trap, with some associated
flinty slate, to a further height of 450 feet.

I believe exactly the same order is observed
in the analogous range of Billingen, near
Sköfde, and at Mosseberg, near Falköping ;
but that the successive strata are thicker than
at Kinnekulle. It is remarkable that in all
these localities, the same as at Hunneberg, the
stratification has apparently not been at all
disturbed by the intrusion of the trap.

The limestone of Kinnekulle is much employed for building and ornamental purposes :
specimens of it may be seen not only at Gö-
thenborg, but at much more distant places, as
for instance, at Hamburg. It takes a tolerable
polish ; and the *Orthocerarites*, with which it
abounds, add much to its beauty, from the
variety produced by the different sections of
their chambers, which, as well as the Siphuncle,
are usually cased with crystallized carbonate

of lime. Any of the quarries on the sides of this mountain will supply the Geologist not only with this fossil, but also with abundant varieties of small *Trilobites*, and *Battus*; and if he be industrious or fortunate, with still rarer specimens. Very fair quarters may be obtained on the mountain, at a farmhouse called Rosætter: and about three miles from it, to the North, are the large Alum works of Honsætter.

In addition to the localities here described, a similar limestone is quarried at Omsberg, on the Eastern shore of Lake Wettern; it is of a greenish grey colour, and among other fossils seems to contain many strongly striated *Terebratulæ*. According to Hisinger's map of this mountain, a nucleus of granite replaces the trap of Kinnekulle: a little to the South of Omsberg is an interesting tract of Keuper sandstone.

The line of the Götha Canal, between Lakes Wettern and Roxen, passes through transition rocks: and many good fossils were obtained

at Motala, Husbyfjöl, Berg, &c. during the
formation of the canal. I did not, however,
see any quarry, or good section, along this
line; and the only organic remains I found
in any quantities, were the usual *Battus*. Besides these localities, it will be seen on referring
to Hisinger's map, that there are numerous
other isolated patches of transition rocks,
dispersed throughout this portion of Sweden,
that stretch across in a direction S. E., and
N. W. in a sort of band terminating in the
islands of Gottland and Öland.

Can we doubt that these rocks of a similar
geological age, and containing similar fossils,
were once more or less continuous? and that
subsequently, devastating floods have swept
away the greater part of them, and denuded the
fundamental Gneiss? In the case of Kinnekulle, and the other trap hills, we may imagine
that the superfused igneous rock protected
the strata from these destructive forces: their
position with reference to the Gneiss, and their

undisturbed bedding, forbidding us to suppose they can have been elevated above the reach of their action.

As a further evidence of the long and violent action of water over this district, posterior to the deposition of the latest rocks, though prior to the habitation of man, may be mentioned the well known Oasar, or Sand-oasar, heaps of gravel and pebbles, intermixed with large boulders, more or less rounded, and undoubtedly derived from the older Scandinavian rocks. This formation of Baltic boulders, as it is now generally called, or *Terrains de transport*, according to French nomenclature, extends to the Southward, across the Baltic, far into central Germany; and in breadth, from the Eastern coast of Scotland and Norfolk, up to Moscow. But in this portion of Sweden, so near to its native seat, it attains great thickness, and forms (as its name implies) islands, and terraces, on which villages are built, and roads are carried. It has been thought that a

certain regularity of direction in the outline
of these transported heaps may be observed;
as well as some approach to a stratification, or
lamination of their contents : I do not dispute
the facts, but I cannot confirm them by my
own limited observation.

I have already alluded to the enormous
deposit of shells, identical with those still found
in the adjoining sea, which may be seen at
various spots near Uddevalla; but especially
on the hill of Capellbacken, half a mile from
the town, where they attain a height of 190
feet above the sea.   At Jonserud near Göthen-
borg, is a similar deposit, but of more limited
extent, and only fifty or sixty feet above the
sea.

The Southern Province of Scania is a very
interesting district, especially to an English
Geologist; from a great portion of it consisting
of chalk and greensand, which are so beautifully developed in our own country.   Unfortunately, however, the comparison of these

distant localities of the same formations is rendered less satisfactory by the almost total absence of any good sections. The shores of Scania are very low, presenting every appearance of having recently emerged from the sea; as various independent facts warrant us in concluding to be the case.

The Geologist must not expect to find the bold cliffs of Dover, or the Isle of Wight. True chalk, in fact, is scarcely to be seen; or only at Charlottenlund, and Östratorp, on the Southern coast, and at Sallerup, near Malmö. About a couple of miles to the South of Malmö, at a place called Lim-hamn *(i. e.* "Lime haven")* they dig up on the shore, and burn, small masses of a greyish, hard, chalk marl. Among the heaps collected at the kiln, I found two or three species of *Terebratulæ,* (chiefly *ovalis* and *curvirostris*) two or three *Spatangi (Cor anguinum)* a shark's tooth, said to be uncommon ; *Ostrea vesicularis ;* and numerous stalks of a species of *Siphonia.*

A little to the East of Ystad is the principal deposit of Greensand; but here also good sections are sadly wanting. The surface of the country is low, and undulating, covered with a loose sandy soil, intermixed with the usual boulders of Gneiss, granite, and syenite. Several oval Tumuli, or Barrows, rise in this plain, and are universally ascribed to Odin by the natives. A small stream has cut through the loose soil, to a depth of about thirty feet; and turns two mills at Svenstorp and Köpinge Mölla, which are celebrated localities for Scanian fossils. It is, however, useless to expect to obtain any good specimen there now, unless there happen to be a quarry accidentally opened, or the Tourist be prepared to employ men for two or three days to dig.

At Svenstorp Mölla, below the loose sand are seen thin layers of hardish stone, with the dark green grains of silicate of iron, common to the Greensand formation. The pretty little *Pecten pulchellus*, and a few fragments and casts of others, were all the fossils I saw there. At Köpinge, the only place to search for specimens is in some pits on the side of a sand hill, made to keep the potatoes. After digging and delving there for two or three hours, I only succeeded in discovering a quantity of *Dentalia*, and small *Belemnites*; with a few *Pectens*, and some indistinguishable fragments that crumbled to pieces immediately. Hisinger's "Lethæa Svecica," however, and Nilsson's "Petrificata Suecana," show that much better success has been obtained here, by employing better means.

In the neighbourhood of Christianstad are several noted spots for fossils, such as Mörby, the island of Ifö, Kjugestrand, and Balsberg: all of which Hisinger classes as chalk, though there is not the slightest appearance of chalk any where near, but only sand: and the fossils, as far as I am aware, would agree equally with the Greensand. I staid there several days, and saw enough to convince me that there are a hundred spots as favourable for fossil hunting, as those that have acquired a name. The district has been little visited, and is somewhat difficult to penetrate from the abundance of Lakes : it is, however, on their shores that the fossils are chiefly found; as there are no quarries, and few artificial excavations of any kind.

By far the best locality for fossils that I visited in Scania, is Ignaberga, about eighteen miles to the North-east of Christianstad. Near this village is an extensive deposit of shells and corals, so pure and free from foreign substances, as to be burned for the lime, employed in household uses, being considered too expensive for manure. In the largest quarry that I examined, about a mile from Ignaberga, I found the bed worked to a depth of thirty feet. The greater part of this enormous mass of shells, consisted of broken fragments : but in the course of a few hours I spent in several of these quarries, I collected a great number of the pretty little *Cranium striatum* (including four or five specimens with both valves quite perfect); many *Belemnites (mucronatus,* and *mammillatus)* also quite perfect, but without any trace of an Operculum; several beautiful *Terebratula Lyra, Ter. spathulata,* &c.; many *Pectens* and *Plagiostoma;* numerous spines and plates of *Cidaris; Chama Cornu Arietis; Podopsis truncata;* various *Oysters;* and an infinity of small *Corallines.* A workman gave me three or four small shark's teeth; and told me they had thrown many away.

From Ignaberga to Hör is about twenty miles; the road is hilly, and pretty for so flat a country as Scania: some basaltic rocks on the way deserve notice. A Scotchman keeps the inn at Hör,—where are Scotchmen not to be found? and though he has fallen too much into the filthy and uncomfortable habits of his adopted country, still his house affords rather more comfort than the dirty hovels met with

in this part of Sweden. The Scanians have
the character among their Swedish and Danish
neighbours, of being the filthiest, coarsest,
most uncivil and treacherous people, of the
Scandinavian race. The picture may be a
little overcharged: but I must confess that
during my fortnight's tour among them, I
met with much to confirm, and very little to
gainsay, these severe charges. And as for
eatables, even after my long experience of
Norway, I scarcely know how I should have
lived, if it had not been for eels, which, cold
or hot, formed my daily dinner and supper.

Immediately to the South of Hör, and as far
as the Lake Ringsjön, lies a tract of lowish,
undulating hills, in the midst of the Gneiss
rocks. They are composed of a more or less
coarse sandstone, often containing rounded
pebbles of quartz, so as to form a silicious brec-
cia; and much resembling our millstone grit.
Like it also, this stone is extensively quarried
for grinding-stones; and in certain spots con-

tains abundant impressions of plants. Vegetable matter is indeed disseminated throughout the rock; but nowhere so plentifully as to constitute coal. I found many pieces of carbonized wood; tolerable specimens of two or three of the Ferns, named after Professor Nilsson, and peculiar, I believe, to this locality; many Calamites; and a few of the leaves, which are said to belong, and have every appearance of belonging, to Dicotyledonous trees. The geological age of this formation is not yet determined; though by many it is referred to the Wealden: it appears to lie between the Lias and Greensand; that is, if it be allowed that the Coalfield of Höganäs really belong to the Lias, as a few trifling fossils would seem to indicate.

The English coal owner need not fear the rivalry of the Höganäs mines, which are situated about twelve miles to the North of Helsingborg, near the entrance of the Sound. I was assured by the very intelligent chief engineer, named Peders, that there are only five seams

of coal, from one to seven inches thick, which
last is the thickest yet discovered! The greatest
depth they have actually worked is about forty-
five fathoms; but they have bored nearly twice
as deep, and found likely strata, when the
water came in upon them, and stopped their
progress. It could not possibly.pay to work so
poor beds, if they did not also raise excellent
clay for fire bricks. The coal is not only defi-
cient in quantity, but in quality: it seems im-
perfectly carbonized, and contains much sulphur. Few impressions of plants have been
found in the associated beds; but such as have
been met with, are mostly curious and peculiar,
and have been sent to Stockholm. In examining the heaps at the pit mouth, I saw nothing
but the stems of calamites, much resembling
those of our own Culm measures, but without
fronds; and no Ferns, &c.

Before quitting Scania, the geologist should
make a point of visiting Lund, the seat of an
ancient archbishopric, and a considerable mo-

dern University. In the Museum belonging to
the latter is a good geological collection; but a
much more instructive and interesting one is
possessed by the distinguished Professor Nilsson,
to whom the Tourist who seeks for information
should certainly endeavour to obtain an introduction. His collection contains the best specimens of almost all the fossils found in Sweden:
and the intelligent Professor's accompanying
observations render their examination doubly
agreeable and improving.

Having mentioned the very unsatisfactory
manner in which the chalk appears in Scania,
I cannot but advertise the dabbler in geology
(for the experienced geologist will be aware of
the fact) that he will find this formation much
better developed on the opposite coast of Denmark, at Stevenbklint, Faxöe, and in the
Island of Möen. These localities have been
generally described, with great accuracy, by
Mr. Lyell. The Museum at Copenhagen possesses excellent specimens of the organic re-

mains found there, which though agreeing in
the main with the fossils of our own chalk,
afford many peculiarities. In the Copenhagen
Museum, for instance, may be seen fine and
perfect specimens of the large *Trochus Danicus*,
and *Nautilus Danicus;* as well as the many
corals peculiar to the Faxöe bed; also the
pretty little *Magus (Terebratula?) pumila*, abundant at Faxöe, but rare elsewhere. There
are, likewise, in the same collection, many
good examples of the Scanian fossils; and the
largest and the most perfect *Olenus Tessini* yet
discovered.

Those who are interested in the most recent
formations, which either immediately preceded,
or were contemporaneous with, the first appearance of man in these parts, will be much grati-
fied by the inspection of the abundant specimens
from what Dr. Forchhammer calls " the Quaternary Formation," as being subsequent to
the " Tertiary." In the latter no trace of
man's works is found; in the former, pieces of

rude pottery, boats, and household implements, are occasionally discovered. Great part of Denmark consists of this formation, none of the Danish Continent being older than the chalk: but the North-west coast of Jutland, near Ven-cyssel, appears to be the most favourable point for its observation. There, at the promontory of Robsnæs, Dr. Forchhammer has found these recent strata, which are usually horizontal, suddenly thrown up to an angle of 70°: and exhibiting a thickness that he cannot calculate less than 8000 feet.

Perhaps the most interesting phænomenon connected with the "Quaternary" deposits is the occurrence of Märtöfv, or Marine Peat; which seems to form a connecting link between our Peat Mosses, and the German Brown coal: the different degrees of compression alone, apparently, causing relative distinctions of character.

If the geologist be desirous to render his survey of this part of Europe still more complete,

he will find the Islands of Bornholm (of which
Dr. Forchhammer has published a map and
account) and of Gottland, well deserving his
attention. The former possesses a considerable
deposit of coal, supposed to be of the same age
as that of Höganäs : in the latter, there is an
extensive formation of Transition limestone,
with a peculiar sandstone, and a dubious Oolite,
all of them rich in fossils, of which several appear to be confined to that Island.

CHAPTER XII.

IF, in the above slight sketches of my visits to Scandinavia, I have at all succeeded in conveying to the reader an adequate idea of the impressions they made on me, he will readily understand that I look back to them with feelings of pleased and grateful recollection. The scenery of Norway is highly picturesque ; to

the lover of the wild and grand it is pre-emi-
nently attractive. Many of its features, as,
for instance, its Fjords, are peculiar: and no
less so are its moral and political features, its
modes of living and domestic habits.

There is, in fact, a freshness and strangeness about the country and its inhabitants,
which to one only conversant with those nations
whose more marked peculiarities have been
worn off by constant intercourse, is highly de-
lightful. In such a country, and among such
a people, it will be readily understood that a
thousand details of beauty will daily be seen, a
thousand adventures of interest or amusement
be met with, which though contributing greatly
to the Tourist's every day's enjoyment, it is
scarcely possible, or might even appear trifling
to commit to paper.

Then what I confess to be always a great
addition to the recommendations of a Tour in
my eyes, is the honest and kindly character of
the Norwegians. Who is there, that has tra-

velled through central Europe for instance, that
has not felt it to be a great drawback to his
pleasures, to be made daily aware of the un-
friendly spirit with which an Englishman is
usually regarded by the French, or to see himself cheated and laughed at by a people whom
he cannot help so much despising, as the
Italians !

In Norway, on the contrary, the English
character stands very high: and it will be the
Englishman's own fault, if he be not both
respected and liked. In the few instances I
knew of my countrymen getting into serious
quarrels with the natives, it was invariably
the Englishman's fault; and when it did not
arise from misapprehension (in consequence
of his ignorance of the language, as well as
the laws and customs of the land in which
he was travelling) was sure to be connected
with that besetting sin of Britons, the determination to flog the little grass-fed ponies of
Norway up and down its precipitous hills, at

the same rate that our powerful horses carry the mail along our magnificent roads. I have already expressed my sentiments as to the unfairness, and unkindness, and I may add, the impolicy of this conduct; for the Norwegian will not tamely bear this treatment of his beast: and if the stranger persist in it, he will be sure to get into constant altercations at every Station, and eventually most probably into an unpleasant scrape, as the laws are sufficiently severe on this subject.

I also heard of a few instances where Englishmen fancied themselves cheated by the Norwegians: some of these instances I had an opportunity of investigating, and satisfied myself that the supposed grievance was founded solely on their own inability to understand, or be understood by, the natives; or that they were imposed upon by their own servant, in whose hands their ignorance completely placed them. I do not mean to assert that trifling instances of overcharge never occur, in the towns espe-

cially: but I can only say that during eight
or ten months I have spent in Norway, tra-
versing its entire length and breadth, I never
met with any thing that could be called a
serious case of imposition or deception. What
foreigner can say as much for England?

So much for my experience of the lower
and middle classes, with whom the Tourist,
merely passing through the country, mostly
comes in contact. But I have also mixed
a good deal with the upper ranks of Norwegians: and ungrateful indeed should I be, if
I did not add my humble testimony not only
of the admiration and affection they universally
expressed towards my country, but also of
the kindness and hospitality they showed to
myself individually.

An observant Englishman can scarcely visit
any land without being impressed with the
conviction that a large portion of the liberties
of the world is at stake in the safety or fall
of our diminutive Island: but in Norway

more especially will he be made aware of the
universal conviction of the people, that England is the Palladium of their liberty and inde-
pendence. What a change of relative position
a few centuries have produced, when that
mighty Empire which now broods, as it were,
over so many millions from India to Canada,
should be implored to grant a scanty portion
of its protecting pinions to the not degenerate
descendants of a people who once ravaged her
shores, and seized her throne, at will!

I must, however, confess that, attached as
I became to the country and its inhabitants,
my admiration is not so indiscriminate, as to
blind me to its deficiencies, or to view it as an
El dorado for emigrants, or to recommend it
for imitation in all its institutions, as a late
and intelligent Tourist has done, whose exagge-
rated partiality is universally laughed at by
the Norwegians themselves.

I do not doubt that a certain number of
steady and industrious young men, with suffi-

cient capital to purchase a small estate, might
provide themselves and their families with all
the common necessaries of life, more easily in
Norway, than in an old and overstocked country like England. But then, it must be borne
in mind that but few could be so accommo-
dated. The extent of uncultivated land in
Norway is indeed great; but its position and the
circumstances of its climate, render it also un-
cultivatable: the failure of the crops for so
many successive seasons, in many of the higher
Straths, proves that the point of profitable cultivation in an average of years has been passed.

The quantity of good arable land is mostly
confined to the Vallies, and is small. A patch
of such land is indispensable: for, in Norway,
there is no opportunity of selling one article
of produce to purchase another: every master
of a family must produce every thing that
he requires, on his own land. The very trifling
superfluities he will have to dispose of, after
feeding all those by whose labour they are

obtained, must go to procure the few articles of colonial produce he can afford to consume, and to pay his taxes.

Then, for six or seven months of the year, no out-door work can be done : for the other half of the year, I have already indicated what incessant and severe labour must be encountered. An intending emigrant should therefore well reckon the cost of these various drawbacks, before he rashly quits any situation in which he is but tolerably well off. The demand for casual labour is too precarious to be depended on; and the work expected is both too severe, and too poorly requited, to tempt an English labourer from even the most poverty-stricken of our districts.

In winter time there is no call for extra labour, beyond that which is supplied by each Farmer's own family. During the harvest work can generally be procured, at the rate of from 5d. to 8d. besides victuals, for a day of sixteen hours of hard toil. Sometimes

taskwork can be got : I found the men paid
thus at Rogstad, in the autumn of 1837. They
received 16 skillings (or about 7*d.*) for every
thirty sheaves of barley, that they .cut, and
tied, and fixed on the tall stakes, which are
placed for this purpose at proper intervals,
throughout every corn field in Norway. Eight
sheaves are stuck, one above the other, on each
stake : but a man must work very hard, and
the corn must stand well up and thick, for
him to be able to earn an English shilling.
He is besides fed; which may be reckoned
about 5*d.* more : at least the men who are
employed to look after the floating timber,
where it is delayed by Fosses or shallows,
usually receive a mark, or 10*d.* a day, without
victuals, or half a mark, if with food.

The only labourers in Norway who can be
considered well off are the " Housemen ;" a
small number of whom are attached to every
considerable farm. They have a house and
plot of ground, with summer pasturage, and

the use of the adjoining forest for timber and
fuel, rent free : for these advantages they are
bound to give a certain number of days' labour
to the proprietor, whenever he requires it.
These situations are however so few, and so
much sought after, that the most industrious
labourer has usually long to wait before he can
obtain one.

One of my chief objections to the Norwegian character is in a great measure connected
with this very abundance of the commonest
necessaries of life which the owners of the
land certainly can command. The comparative
facility with which their sensual wants to a
certain extent can be satisfied, makes them
pay far too much attention to the body, too
little to the mind. Eating and drinking are
of infinitely too great importance in Norway :
while intellectual pleasures seem very little
regarded.

The power of reading is very general, through
a compulsory system I shall shortly have occa-

sion to allude to; but except in the towns, where the newspapers afford the chief field for its exercise, little advantage seems to be made of it. In the country, and during the summer, at least, it is very rare to see any Norwegian, of any station, employed in reading: and the very scanty supply of books that a Norwegian house ever contains, proves the fact.

It is, no doubt, also dependent on this necessity for constant labour, that the Norwegians appear to have no peculiar sports, or country amusements whatever. I never saw them engaged in any pastime: nor could I hear of any national game. When even they fish, or shoot, it is done entirely for the pot, not for pleasure. This is not to be wondered at. It is easy to understand that after a week of such incessant toil, as their position renders imperative, rest alone is a sufficient enjoyment; and the absence of exertion, with the sedentary relaxations of tobacco and spirits, all that the body requires.

But how fares it with the mind, under such a system ? how can the intellectual energies be exerted, and improved, enlarged, exalted by that exertion ? how in short can all that dignifies man above the beasts that eat, and fatten, and perish, and that makes him partaker of a better and higher life than that of mere physical existence, be adequately promoted ? It is very possible, indeed probable, that during their long winters these Northern people may both read and amuse themselves, much more than they do during their brief summers. But it is impossible that their amusements even at that period, as well as their general national character, should not be stamped with more or less of the unintellectual features impressed on them by the peculiarities of their daily life.

The necessity of providing for their daily existence makes them live only for the present, not for posterity. If they were swept away from the face of the earth, the Norwegians would leave behind them no monument of human skill, or labour, or intellect, to tell another generation that a great people had so long tenanted the wide extent of Scandinavia. Nature's monuments would indeed still remain: Norway's Fjelder and Fjords would still claim the homage of the admirer of the sublime and beautiful. But no work of public utility or ornament—(its two or three cathedrals can scarcely be reckoned an exception)—no achievement in Science or Literature, wherewith the human mind of one period holds converse with the mind of all times, would exist to excite the regrets and admiration of the future wanderer on these shores. Not only the mighty empires of Egypt and Rome, but even the petty states of Greece, have left records of their existence, which must endure as long as the Arts are cultivated, or Letters are preserved, among men: whereas a single century of oblivion would obliterate all that the Norwegians have yet done for Posterity!

By many perhaps, their famous Constitution
of 1814* will be considered ἱe most valuable
contribution that the Norwegians have rendered to the liberties of their fellow men, as
well as the best claim to their admiration.   It
bears evident marks of the haste with which
it was concocted, having been ostensibly prepared, within a very few days, on the exigency
of the moment: although doubtless it was
mainly modelled on the many previous attempts
at Constitutions, that originated in the French
Revolution; and in fact, is said to have been
in embryo existence some time before.

* I dare not affix the date of the month, as well as of the
year, this being even yet a subject of great and bitter debate.
The Constitution was proclaimed by the Norwegians on the
17th of May, 1814: it received its sanction from the King,
and assembled Storthing, on the 4th of November following.
Accordingly, the former anniversary is celebrated with great
enthusiasm by the People, to show that they consider they owe
their liberties to themselves alone; the latter is observed by
the Government and its subordinates, in maintenance of the
doctrine that their authority, if not derived from, at least requires the concurrence of the Sovereign.

It is essentially democratic; too much so, it would seem, to be long compatible with the existence of a Monarchy, in any but so small a kingdom as Norway, and in such peaceful times as it has hitherto encountered. Were it exposed to the test of extended power, or wealth, or foreign aggression, my opinion is that it would fail, or at least require great modifications. Indeed, all well-informed Norwegians with whom I have conversed, confess that it contains many faults both of omission and of commission. At the same time, it has in the main worked so well hitherto, that they naturally fear lest in altering any of the objectionable parts, they might lose some of the essentials.

Their attachment to the " Ground-Law," as it is called, and their jealousy of the Swedes, with whom they are now linked, after having been so often and so long at war with them, are equally excessive. At the same time, with all their democratic tendencies and their antipathy to Sweden, the great mass of the Norwegians have uniformly expressed, both publicly and privately, great attachment to their Sovereign, Carl Johann, as he styles himself, though christened Jean Baptiste Julian Bernadotte, and raised by his talent and fortune to the dignities of Marshal of France and Prince of Ponte Corvo. His manners are highly attractive; and during the last winter (of 1838-39) that he spent at Christiania, he personally won golden opinions from all ranks; although not a whit the more for that, would they accede to the propositions made to the then sitting Storthing, in his name.

The power of the Executive certainly appears to be too much limited: every thing that can fence in, and secure the liberties of the people, has been devised: but many other most material points have been overlooked. No one connected with the Ministry, in any degree, or with the Court, or in the receipt of a pension, can be elected to the Storthing, which, be it

remembered, is both Lords and Commons. By
the sixty-second article of the Ground-Law it
is provided, (it is written in French, as well as
in Norsk,) " Les Membres du Conseil d'Etat,
et les fonctionnaires employés à leurs bureaux ;
les Officiers de la Cour et ses pensionnaires ne
pourront être nommés Représentans."

By this overstrained jealousy, the Storthing
is not only deprived of the talents of many of
the ablest and best men ; but its labours are
often greatly protracted, and the business in-
completely and slovenly performed, which might
be obviated by the presence of men possessed
of official information, and official habits of
business.

The time that intervenes between the
sessions of the Storthing, is another serious
objection. From the same jealousy, nothing of
importance is allowed to be done except by the
Storthing ; and as it only meets once in every
three years, on the first of February, useful and
necessary measures are often grievously delayed.

This inconvenience is already much felt : and
will be yearly more sensible, with the progres-
sive advance of the country ; until at length it
will imperatively require alteration. The objection is, that on account of the distances
that many of the Members have to travel, and
the badness of the roads, it would be impossible
for them to meet oftener. But let them con-
tinue to improve their communications, as it is
their duty to do, and this objection will gradually lose its force : while the Members being so
liberally paid, that most of them save money
during their attendance, the worldly circumstances even of the poorest are not injured by it.

The Criminal Law of Norway confessedly
needs great improvement : it is both defective,
and far too severe, for modern ideas of legislation. The principal labour of the last Session
of the Storthing (in 1839) was its correction
and melioration. Much difference of opinion
existed as to the extent of improvement effected
by the New Law : however, the king refused

his assent to it, and thus this desirable reform is put off for at least three years. The king has the power of refusing his assent to any measure twice: but if the same identical measure passes three successive Storthings, it then becomes *ipso facto* the law of the land. This was the way in which the hereditary nobility of Norway was abolished, against the strenuous opposition of the king and court.

Carl Johann's motive, in withholding his assent to the proposed alterations in the Criminal Law, was understood to be his wish to assimilate them to the improvements intended to be introduced into the Swedish Code by the Diet now (1840) sitting at Stockholm. Ever since he came to the throne, it has been his evident and natural object to amalgamate, as far as possible, the two nations so unexpectedly submitted to his sway. How far he will succeed with such very discordant materials, as he has to deal with, remains to be proved, but I think may be guessed.

It is difficult to imagine two people so nearly connected, by position and origin, more dissimilar than the Swedes and Norwegians. In Norway is a nearly pure democracy, with a very limited king as its chief magistrate : no nobility: a perfectly free press : an equality of succession among the sons to the paternal property ; and consequently an equalization of estates, and those small. In Sweden on the contrary, is a powerful monarchy ; a very numerous nobility ; with the feudal law of succession. The Norwegians are consequently, (speaking generally) a sturdy, but rather rough, race of honest republicans : while the Swedes, it must confessed, possess many more of the graces and accomplishments, contaminated also, unfortunately, with the vices of civilization.

It is sufficiently clear which of these two dissimilar states is most likely to find favour in a king's eyes, in his attempt to blend them together. However, I feel well convinced, that if their institutions are to be assimilated, Sweden must meet Norway much more than half-way. The sturdy democrat is not likely to yield all to the more polished aristocrat: besides, the superiority of the Norwegian institutions, in many respects, and their evident influence on the national prosperity, are too decided, not to be palpable to both people.

Carl Johann has renewed his so often rejected proposition, to be discussed (and rejected) in the next Storthing, to give the Sovereign an absolute Veto. He supports his proposal with great earnestness, but not very conclusive reasoning. Another wish of his is to have the power of Naturalization, which has hitherto been denied him, from a fear lest he should fill all the offices with needy Swedish Nobles. By the Ground-Law none but a Norwegian can occupy a post in the Norwegian Government: but if the king possessed this power of Naturalization, he could confer them upon any foreigner; that is, provided he be not a Monk or a Jew; for on the very first page of this ultra-liberal Con-

stitution it is decreed (Art. 2.) "Les Ordres des
Jesuites et des Moines ne sont point tolérés
dans le Royaume : les Juifs sont aussi désor-
mais, comme ci-devant, exclus du Royaume."

A third point, upon which Carl Johann used
to feel very strongly, he seems to have at
length given up; rather, most probably, from
seeing the impossibility of ever carrying it,
than from any change in his convictions or
sentiments : I mean the restoration of an
hereditary nobility. However natural, and,
as it would seem to us, almost necessary an
adjunct to an hereditary monarchy, such a
class may be, it hardly could exist long with
the Norwegian Law that divides every father's
property in equal shares among his sons, with
half portions to the daughters.

The necessary effect of this law is to bring
down the great mass of properties to an average
size capable of maintaining a family, by the
labour of its members. Some little variation
in amount is necessarily produced by the

occasional centring of several properties in one, or the marriage of an heiress, or the operation of the Odel-barnsret.* But these circumstances only interfere for a time with the natural effect of the Law, which has practically reduced the great majority of Norwegian estates to this standard. Much below it, they evidently cannot fall: as if a son's share be not sufficient to maintain him, with the severest labour, he must sell it for what he can get, and endeavour to support himself in some other way.

* The term Odel, evidently nearly allied to the Teutonic Adel, or Edel, signifies an independent proprietor, free from all suit or service or acknowledgement whatever, to any superior. And the "Odel-barnsret" is an ancient privilege belonging to this class, whereby the eldest son may (if he is enabled by marriage or any other means so to do) pay off his brothers' and sisters' shares, at a fair valuation, and retain the family property; or in case of sale, the next of kin may claim the family estate, within five years, upon repayment of the purchase money, and the sums expended on improvements. Such is the natural prejudice in favour of retaining properties in the same line, which no legislation can utterly eradicate, that notwithstanding the strictest enactments, the valuations are said to be invariably made greatly in favour of the eldest son.

Such a state of things, however, is clearly incompatible with an hereditary nobility; the essence of which is not only the preference secured to one son over the rest, but the pre-eminence of its possessor over the inferior ranks by whom he is surrounded. In corroboration of this it may be mentioned, that when the hereditary nobility were abolished, although "Fidei Commissa," or entails, were then under certain circumstances permitted, yet there were only three noble families in Norway, and those of foreign extraction.

At Carl Johann's advanced time of life (he was born in January, 1764) he cannot possibly expect to effect many more changes: what may be the fate of his Son is open to much speculation. Many contingencies that we can foresee as probable, and doubtless many more which no human foresight can guess at, may arise to influence still more important destinies than those of the Sovereign of Scandinavia.

Prince Oscar has hitherto kept much aloof from public affairs; or rather, it is said, has been so kept by the inexplicable jealousy of his Father. But he is understood to possess considerable talents, with a more liberal system of politics than his Sire; and has at any rate made himself extremely beloved among all classes. His accession, therefore, would, I doubt not, be very popular: and I do not believe there is the slightest foundation for the strange notion, entertained by a late Traveller in Sweden, before referred to, namely, of a partition between the two lately united kingdoms, which would give Norway to Prince Oscar, and restore Sweden to the old line of the Vasas. I am convinced that no such idea exists among any considerable party in the whole Scandinavian Peninsula.

I much fear, however, that there may be far more foundation for Mr. Laing's suspicion that Russia would be likely to take the first favourable opportunity of seizing parts, at least, of

Sweden and Norway. A very general appre-
hension of some such design is certainly entertained in the North; although no one,
that I ever heard of, attempts to justify it
on his plea, that she requires them for a
port, to enable her to supply her subjects more
conveniently with colonial articles! On the
same plea any highwayman might justify his
measures to supply himself with what he
wanted.

The Northern Bear is indeed a fearful
neighbour: and not only the general policy
of Russia, but her particular measures in
Finmark and Nordland, as well as her lately
constructed fortifications within sight of Stockholm, may well rouse the fears of so weak a
power as Norway. Her army is but 12,000
men: and though the Norwegians are undoubtedly brave, they have not a military turn; at
least, whether seen on guard, or at their annual
exercise, they have any thing but a military
tournure. They are much better adapted for

sailors : but their present marine is absolutely nothing.*

In short, they must, in case of Russian aggression, trust to foreign assistance; and England is the country to which they universally look, as, I trust, they would not look in vain. To this aid, backed by the proverbial courage of mountaineers and the natural difficulties of the country, and above all protected by the righteous Judge of a righteous cause, will the liberties of this interesting country owe their preservation, should they ever unfortunately be attacked. I confess that my own strong impression was, that the last Norwegian would die on the last mountain side, sooner than yield the liberty he prizes so highly : but I was sorry to see that such was not the conviction of the best informed Norwegians themselves.

It is not very easy for a stranger to acquire

* Every Norwegian is liable to serve, for five or seven years, up to the age of twenty-seven for the army, and thirty for the navy : after which age, he is exempt, except in case of invasion.

altogether just, or perfectly accurate notions of
the internal economy of so peculiar a country,
as Norway. But from what I could observe of
the constitution and working of their adminis-
trative system, it appeared to me well adapted
to their social state. Norway is divided for all
civil purposes into the four Stifts or Provinces
of Agershuus (or Christiania), Trondhjem, Bergen, and Christiansand; which are subdivided
into seventeen Amts, or Counties; and these
again into forty-four Fogderies, or Bailiwicks.
Each of these is respectively presided over by
an Amtmand, and a Foged. All the higher
duties of the magistracy, the collection of the
revenue, the care of the roads, the superintendence of the postmasters and innkeepers, and
such like, devolve upon the Amtmen, and
Fogeds. Under them is a Lensman in every
parish :· he is usually the most respectable and
intelligent man of the district; and it is to
him that the Traveller should have recourse,
in case he meet with any difficulty, or in-

jury. Such of the Bönder as are members of the Storthing, are usually chosen from among the Lensmen.

There are no ambulatory judges of assize as with us; but in the principal towns are judicial courts, with a supreme court in Christiania, called the " Höjeste Ret," from whose decisions, I believe, there is no appeal, although the judges in that, as in every court, are liable to have actions brought against them, not only for corrupt judgments but also for ignorance, or incompetency. This responsibility is by no means nominal : they are often severely fined, or even deposed.

Throughout the length and breadth of the land are numerous Sörenskrivers, whose office is of the greatest practical importance, in consequence of the Norwegian law of succession, so often mentioned. The Sörenskriver superintends the valuation and division of property, to insure its just distribution among the heirs of every deceased proprietor—no trifling matter—besides executing various subordinate legal duties.

But the most peculiar court of justice in Norway is that named "Forligelses-Commission;" that is, Court of Reconcilement, or Arbitration. There is such a court in every parish: it consists of three persons, chosen by the parishioners, of whom the Priest is almost invariably the chief, with the Church-wardens, or the Lensman, as his Assessors. Every intended litigation must in the first instance be submitted to this Commission, before it can be brought into a higher court. The parties are there personally heard; no professional person being allowed to appear; their evidence is canvassed; and a statement eventually drawn up in which both parties agree, and sign. The Assessors then endeavour to reconcile the parties, usually by proposing some middle course. If both submit to the arbitration, the decision is final: if one demurs, he can carry the case to a higher tribunal, but at the risk of having the expenses to pay, should it be decided against him; and in no case can any fresh facts be brought forward, other than what are contained in the Protocol of the Forligelses-Commission.

Whether any modification of this institution could be beneficially adopted in a country like ours, I am not prepared to say: but I think there can be no doubt, that in a country like Norway it is productive of much more good, than evil, as tending to cut short a great deal of litigation. Strict legal justice is very probably not so much aimed at by a tribunal so constituted, as equity and concord. But a great deal depends upon the personal character of the Assessors, and especially of the Priest: if he be intelligent and pains-taking, the result is highly satisfactory; but if he be old and stupid, as will sometimes be the case, material facts are frequently omitted, and the whole case is sent up in so incomplete, jumbled, and bungling a form, that I have heard Amtmen

declare it is totally impossible to ascertain its
real merits.

The influence of the Clergy is necessarily
very great in all countries : but many circumstances contribute to render it still more
powerful in Norway, than ordinary.   There
being scarcely any resident gentry, the Priest
inevitably concentrates in himself nearly all
the influence attached to superiority of education, manners, knowledge, station, and wealth.
The   Norwegian   Priesthood   are   uniformly
well educated; and, for the country, well en
dowed : in all these points, there is rarely any
one to compete with them in a rural parish,
except perhaps a Sörenskriver, or more distant
Foged.

But   besides   these   important   sources   of
power,   belonging   to   them   as   resident   gentlemen,   the   Priests   possess   a   degree   of   authority,   attached   to   their   ministerial   character,
beyond   that   of   any   other   Protestant   clergy.
The   Scandinavian   Church   is,   of   course,   Lu-

theran : and it is well known that the Lutherans
have thought fit to retain much more both of
the tenets and outward observances of the
Romish Church, than any other body of Pro-
testants that separated from that communion.
Among other things that they have retained,
are the name, the vestments, and a large portion
of the ministerial authority, independent of
the personal character of the Priest.   For thus
he is always called ; and when he celebrates
" the High Mass," as it is also styled, at the
High Altar, he wears a linen vestment, with
an embroidered cross, reaching from his neck
to his feet, precisely similar to those seen in
Roman Catholic chapels.

I confess there is much in the public service
of the Sabbath, as performed in Lutheran
churches, with which I was dissatisfied : there
is far too much singing, far too little reading
of God's Word, far too little common prayer.
As few of my countrymen have had equally
good opportunities of observing the manner

in which the Sabbath duties are discharged in Norway, I will briefly describe the order usually followed, which with little variation is the same in all country parishes.

The men and women are seated, in their best attire, on separate sides of the aisle : a large proportion of the building is invariably occupied by the choir, which is railed off, and contains the High Altar, bearing two huge candlesticks, with a metallic receptacle for the Host, and surmounted by a sort of painted shrine, with gilded figures of the Virgin Mary, and saints; the whole, in short, savouring strongly of Romanism.

At the appointed hour (which is usually late, as there is never a second service in the country at least) an officer called the deacon, but not in holy orders, comes forward to the church rails, and repeats a short exhortation to prayer, concluding with the Lord's Prayer; immediately after which two long Psalms are sung by the entire congregation.

The Priest meanwhile has up to this period been either in the vestry, or kneeling at the Altar, engaged in his own private devotions, but with his back to the people, and taking no share in the service. He now turns round, and from the Altar . reads the Collect and Epistle for the day: the Epistles and Gospels are the same as ours; the collects are different, and somewhat longer. Next follows another Psalm; after which the Priest reads (he ought, if he can, to chant it) the Gospel. A fourth Psalm is sung; during which the Priest mounts the pulpit, and proceeds to deliver a discourse, either extempore or from manuscript, on a subject invariably taken from the Gospel of the day. When he has concluded, he gives out the banns of marriage, together with other notifications, which in a rural parish are often of a very miscellaneous character. The service concludes with a dismission Psalm.

Such is the ordinary routine: but in the country, there usually are, during the summer,

many occasional services, such as baptisms,
administration of the holy communion, mar-
riages, catechizing of the children, &c. which
are all performed during the public service,
and tend greatly to lengthen it; as appropriate Psalms are sung to each, in addition
to the five or six ordinary Psalms, already
mentioned.

The public formularies of the Lutheran
Church decidedly hold the doctrine of Con-
substantiation, with regard to Christ's presence
in the Sacrament of the Last Supper: but the
generality of the Clergy are said (I believe
truly) in reality to entertain opinions on that
point, still further removed from the Romish
Church, and nearer to ours. Those who wish
to receive the Sacrament, merely signify their
intention to the Priest on his coming to the
church, any Sabbath morning: they go with
him into the vestry, where they are " shrived,"
and receive absolution; and then kneeling
round the Altar, receive the Sacrament in

both kinds, as with us, except that the cup
is put to their lips by the Priest, not into their
hands. The Communion service is in the main
very like ours, only shorter: and during its
celebration, the congregation sing appropriate
Psalms.

On the subject of the other Sacrament, the
Lutheran Church holds the doctrine of Bap-
tismal Regeneration very strongly. The Priest
does not take the child into his arms, but
sprinkles it with water, while in the nurse's
arms; and signs it with the sign of the Cross,
both on its forehead, and its breast: the prayers
are very similar to our own. The "Kirke-
Ritual," as I understand it, confines the number of sponsors and witnesses to five: but there
usually are many more, who stand on each side
down the Aisle, and when the ceremony is over
march in procession, one after the other, all
round the Altar (it is called the "Altar-gang")
and as they pass the Priest, severally present
him a small piece of money, for which he makes

a slight obeisance, though appearing to be engaged all the time in his private devotions. All
the friends of the parties, in the Congregation,
next follow, and make a similar offering: the
same also takes place at a Marriage; so that, I
doubt not, a considerable sum often accrues to
the Priest, but, I must say, it has not a good
appearance.

When the children are publicly catechized,
which is frequently done preparatory to confirmation, the two sexes stand down their respective sides of the Aisle, when the Priest, passing
between them, examines them at great length,
both in the words, and the spirit, of Martin
Luther's "Long Catechism." He is, as might
be supposed, very frequently obliged to put the
answers into their mouths.

This preparation for Confirmation is the best
opportunity the poorer members of the Lutheran
Church have of becoming acquainted with
God's will and word. I have shown that no
more of the Bible is publicly read, than what

is contained in the portion of Scripture appointed for the Epistles and Gospels of the respective °Sundays. But previous to Confirmation, each person attends the Priest at his own house, until the latter is quite satisfied with his religious attainments: and as no one can be married, or indeed perform scarcely any civil office, without having been confirmed, it is infinitely more thought of, than in England.

No Religion is allowed to be publicly professed in Norway, but the Established, the Lutheran: and there are practically few, or no Dissenters. There are indeed scattered here and there, throughout the country, principally in the South and West, a few "Hougianers," (see vol. i. page 313,) but they are not only few in number, but also profess to adhere to the Established Church, although they are considered to hold several peculiar tenets, and have private Prayer Meetings in their own houses.

If I were called upon to express my opinion on the subject, I should certainly say that the Norwegians are a generally moral,* but not a religious people : the comparative absence of temptation will partly account for the first; while the hints I have given of their social arrangements, and public religious ministrations will perhaps seem sufficient to explain the latter fact. Those who openly confess a more than ordinary care for the things of another world, and a desire for more frequent and more spiritual ministrations, than the usual service of their Church too generally affords, are here, as elsewhere, stamped with the title of "Helge," or Saints : but they seemed to me few and far between, and chiefly confined to the larger Towns.

The Lutheran Church of Scandinavia (including Denmark, Sweden, and Norway) was one of the few Protestant Communities that retained Episcopacy at the time of the Reformation. There are five Bishops in Norway, and about 340 Parishes. When it is considered that the length of Norway is about 1000 miles, it may easily be imagined of what an enormous size many of these parishes must be. They have been made so in order that the burthen of maintaining the Clergy may fall as lightly as possible upon the scanty and poor population. The Priest receives a fixed amount of corn from each Farm : besides which he has almost always an extensive Glebe, and a good residence, together with the occasional fees before mentioned.

But the necessary consequence of this disproportionate size of the districts intrusted to each Clergyman's care, is a great lack of religious instruction and knowledge. The Parish of Grong, where I resided so long, was upwards of eighty miles in length; with five Chapels. Most of the large Country Parishes contain several Chapels, at great distances from each other : and as it is not the custom in Norway for the Priest ever to perform more than one

Service on the Sabbath, it may be conceived how little opportunity the inhabitants of most retired districts have of publicly praising God, or learning their duty.

The elements of reading and writing, together with Luther's Catechism, are universally taught. In every Parish there are a number of Schoolmasters, proportioned to its size, who during the winter months go from one Farm-house to another, in their respective districts, when all the unconfirmed children of the neighbourhood are compelled to attend. Those who neglect, are not only debarred from the important rite of confirmation; but are also liable to be fined. There is an Annual Visitation of each ecclesiastical district by one of the Priests appointed thereto with the title of "Probst;" when among a great many other similar matters, the list of those who have attended or neglected the schoolmaster is read over, and the delinquents reprimanded or punished: as also the salaries of the schoolmasters

paid. The stipends of the schoolmasters that
I was acquainted with, varied from twelve to
fifteen dollars, (forty-eight to sixty shillings,)
besides which, they are entitled to their board
and lodging, gratis, during their three months'
circuit.

At this same Annual Visitation, the general
state of the Parish is supposed to be accurately
inquired into; the parochial Clergyman gives
a sample of his preaching; and all the candi-
dates for confirmation undergo a very lengthened examination. This latter is always closed
by their singing one or two Psalms: for
Psalmody, as I have shown, entering so much
into their public worship, is necessarily made
almost as much an object of instruction, as
reading. Judging by the only opportunity
I had of observing the Probst's annual Visitation, I should say it is not only an extremely
interesting ceremony, but productive of considerable good; although it cannot be supposed
that the Probst, should be inclined to exercise

any great severity towards his brother Priests, with whom he is in daily habits of intimacy, and above whom he enjoys but a temporary elevation.

I must repeat my conviction, derived from a tolerably extensive intercourse with the rural districts of Norway, that the faculty of reading, thus early and generally acquired, is but little improved in after life. Not only is it extremely rare to see a middle aged Norwegian reading, even on their days of rest; but equally uncommon is the sight of half a dozen volumes in any house. The traveller is so commonly lodged in the room that contains all the Bönder's chief valuables, that he could not help often seeing his books, if he possessed any. In the usual family cupboard I have seldom found other than Psalm books, with an ancient volume of devotions, perhaps, and a copy of the Ground-Law. Bibles are most unfortunately rare: and only twice have I found copies of the beautiful Bible, or Testament,

published in Christiania, by the British and
Foreign Bible Society.

In these remarks, I must of course be
understood as speaking of the interior of Norway : in the Towns, no doubt, there is greater
opportunity, as well as desire, of reading;
though even there, the study of the higher
classes of literature seemed to me confined to
very few, and that chiefly foreign, or in tran-
slations. In the country, the difficulty of
procuring books acts as a great bar to mental
improvement. The " Privileged Handlers,"
who supply the place of shopkeepers throughout the interior, keep only the useful articles,
for which they find the most demand: and
there being no public conveyances, not even a
regular carrier, it is not easy to obtain any
intellectual food from the distant city.

Another grievous impediment to the spread of
information and education, is the absence of any
school superior to the parochial provisions for
elementary instruction before described, except

in the few large Towns. This, coupled with the want of any cheap mode of travelling, necessarily confines the education of the great majority of the children of the Clergy and others of the higher classes resident in the country, to private tuition; which with the parent's many other avocations, cannot but be inadequately performed, even where he has the ability and the inclination for it.

It is impossible that these various circumstances of their social position, with the results that will naturally strike any one as flowing from them, should not have a marked effect on the national character of the Norwegians. I am far from saying that they can all be speedily remedied: some may even think it better for the people that they should remain as they are. I cannot bring myself to believe that such ignorance is bliss: and I am sorry to be led to the conclusion, by such opportunities of forming an opinion as I have had, that the measures of the Storthing are characterised by too niggardly a spirit in these matters : that in short they partake too much of what strikes me to be the leading defect of the national character, namely, an overweening attention to things material, in preference to things moral, or intellectual. There appears to me too democratic an objection to spend money upon any such subjects, too obstinate a jealousy of intrusting any thing to the Executive; which, however it may succeed in effecting a favourable balance sheet, does not contribute to the advance of the national mind, of the moral and intellectual energies of the people.

I do not pretend to understand the intricate subject of the Currency; which, indeed, if we may judge by the disagreement among those who have most studied it, must be a very difficult question. But figures would seem at any rate to show that by the above parsimonious system, the finances of Norway have been brought into a satisfactory state. Its debt is fast disappearing, and its trade is increasing : a

large proportion of the population is in easy
circumstances, as far as the produce of their
lands is concerned. And yet there seems to be
no money in the country : the want of a circulating medium is most grievously felt. Men
who have an abundance of all the common
necessaries of life, find it very difficult to raise
a few shillings: and when they possess some
superfluities, which others are willing enough
to take, they yet find it next to impossible to
obtain ready money, wherewith to purchase
other things they want, or pay their taxes.

A very intelligent Scotchman, who rented
some large farms near Levanger, told me that
this he found to be the great practical evil of
the country. He could raise crops to reimburse
him at the nominal prices of the neighbourhood : but when he came to sell, he was always
obliged to give at the least two years' credit,
even to men of substance ; and at the last, had
such trouble and difficulty to obtain any money,
as to oblige him to give up his farms. The only

way he had of getting cash, was to export his corn in his own vessels to Trondhjem, or some other large town.

There is only one Bank of issue in Norway, stationed at Trondhjem : its paper forms the almost universal circulating medium of the country. For though the standard is silver; coins of that metal are so rare, that, I am sure, I did not altogether see five pounds' worth of silver during two long visits ; and gold I never saw. I never could make out what becomes of the silver raised at Kongsberg : it does not come into the circulation ; and the very scanty supply of spoons and forks, used in Norway, cannot absorb much.

In offering the above general observations on what appeared to me to be the social, moral, and political state of Norway, I have endeavoured briefly, but with all sincerity, to record my impressions of its real character: not feeling it right on the one hand to extenuate what I believed to be faulty in its institutions, while, on the other, still more unwilling to set down aught in malice.

All right minds take an interest in acquiring a correct estimation of the position and social arrangements of the other members of the great family of man. In no other way can this correct estimate be formed by such as have not the opportunity of personally visiting the respective countries, than by comparing together the accounts of the several travellers who have had fair means of judging them. One man may have seen one aspect of the varying phases of society, another a different one: one traveller may have, voluntary or involuntary, prejudices of one sort, another of a totally contrary kind: and the result is the correction of material error in the mind of the intelligent and unbiassed reader.

With this conviction, I ventured to give my impressions, founded on altogether a nine months' residence in Norway, during which I visited a large portion of the country, and mixed extensively with the highest and lowest classes of its inhabitants. I can not by any means boast of peculiar powers of observation: but I am sure I can assert my sincere anxiety to arrive at the truth, and a warm, though not blind, affection both for the people and their land.

Norway must ever possess an especial interest in the eyes of England, far beyond what its narrow bounds, or present rank in the scale of nations, would seem to claim: an interest, derived both from the ancient connexion that formerly subsisted between the two countries, as also the present countenance, and future protection that the one looks to from the other. Norway claims our attention even yet more, from the habits, and institutions of the olden time, which it alone among the old countries of Europe has been able to preserve; and which possess a more than ordinary interest at the present time, when there are some wild spirits at home who dream that a democracy, an equalization of property, the abolition of

all hereditary distinctions (all of which Norway practically possesses to a considerable
extent) would conduce to the improvement
and general benefit of our own nation.

I have endeavoured to show that, though
in a country situated like Norway, such institutions do seem to diffuse a certain degree of
the common necessaries of life, more generally
among all classes, than our more feudal system; yet even in this contracted nation they
have a strong tendency to keep the people
down at a low intellectual level. In a country
like ours (even if such changes could be effected tranquilly, which is impossible) they
would without doubt, destroy every thing that
constitutes the moral and mental greatness of
England.

I trust that the liberties of this small, but
interesting land will not be suffered by us to
be overwhelmed, if ever they be attacked. On
every account, their preservation must be considered a matter of personal importance to

ourselves. The dreaded foe of Norway is the most probable foe of ourselves, in every quarter of the Globe, where we come in contact: the enemy of her liberties is the enemy of those of the whole civilized world. On every side of her overgrown empire, she seems desirous of seizing the deserts of her neighbours, instead of cultivating her own; of adding more and more hordes of savages to the countless millions she already possesses, instead of civilizing and elevating in the scale of being those that have long acknowledged her sway. We have already quite sufficient grounds of jealousy against Russia, at a thousand points, without allowing her to occupy a line of spacious ports, within a short sail of our own Northern shores.

In addition to the moral sources of interest, thus connected with Norway, I have endeavoured (too faintly, I feel and confess,) to bring before the English travelling public, those which are connected with its picturesque physical features, its scenery, its geology; and especially the advantages it holds out to the Angler. All these recommendations Norway offers for a summer's excursion to the Tourist possessed of a healthy frame of mind and body. The former is necessary to appreciate the unsophisticated claims to his admiration that the inartificial state of society in the North presents: the other may be required at first, by the unaccustomed frugality of Norwegian fare, and the want of usual comforts, together with the unavoidable exposure to weather. I think, however, that a short familiarity with such fare will practically convince him that it is more conducive to lightness of spirits and activity of body, than all the mysteries of a Parisian cuisine; while the experience of a few Skydskaffers' accommodations will realize to his convictions what he may before have only acknowledged theoretically, that "Man does in reality want but little here below."

With such feelings, I will only further

express my hope that these pages may be received as a humble contribution to the knowledge of this interesting country and people; and as a grateful, though imperfect, memorial of very many pleasant hours, and of very much personal kindness, for which I am indebted to Norway and Norwegians.

LIST OF SALMON AND TROUT CAUGHT IN 1837.

WHEN.		WHERE.	WHAT.	Total Wt. lbs. oz.
May	30	River Götha, above Trollhettan	2 Trout	5 0
„	31	Ditto, below Trollhettan	5 Ditto	17 12
June	14	Bogstad, near Christiania	10 Ditto	2 0
„	17	Moe, on Lake Mjösen	8 Grayling	5 8
„	22	Near Laurgaard	29 Trout	3 8
„	26	Near Jerkin	25 Ditto	11 0
„	27	Ditto	18 Ditto	9 0
July	10	Steenkjer	2 Salmon	10 8
„	11	Ditto	6 Trout	6 12
„	12	Ditto	1 Ditto, and 1 Salmon of 14lbs.	15 8
„	15	River Namsen, near Grong	4 Salmon, (28, 15, 14, 14lbs.) rose 8	71 0
„	17	Ditto ditto	6 Ditto, (26, 19, 18, 14, 13¾, 4lbs.) rose 8	94 8
„	18	Ditto, near Foseland	1 Ditto; rose 5	15 0
„	19	Ditto, near Grong	3 Ditto; (5, 4, 4lbs.) rose 6	13 0
„	21	Ditto, near Fiskum	1 Ditto; rose 3	11 0
„	22	Ditto, ditto	7 Ditto, (24, 13, 6, 6, 5, 5, 5lbs.) rose 18	64 0
„	24	Ditto, ditto	4 Ditto, (20, 18, 15, 4lbs.) 2 Sea-trout; rose 8 Salmon	62 0
„	25	Ditto, ditto	7 Ditto, (30, 24, 19, 16, 6, 4, 4lbs.) rose 16	103 0
„	26	Ditto, between Fiskum and Foseland	6 Ditto, (31, 15, 14, 5, 4½, 4lbs.) 2 Sea-trout, (5, 2lbs.) rose 9 Salmon	80 8
„	27	Ditto, near Grong	7 Ditto, (24, 7, 5, 4, 4, 4lbs.) 1 Sea-trout, (6lbs.) rose 10 Salmon	58 0

Date	Location	Catch	lbs	oz
July 28	Ditto, near Fossland	5 Ditto, (24, 16, 14, 5, 4lbs.) 1 Sea-trout; rose 12 Salmon	64	0
" 29	Ditto, near Fiskum	4 Ditto, (16, 15, 5, 4lbs) 1 Sea-trout, (6lbs.) rose 6 Salmon	46	8
" 31	Ditto, ditto	2 Ditto, (28, 27lbs.) 1 Sea-trout; rose 5 Salmon	56	0
August 1	Ditto, ditto	5 Ditto, (30, 24, 22, 21, 20lbs.) rose 12	117	0
" 2	Ditto, ditto	4 Ditto, (22, 21, 14, 12lbs.) rose 10	69	0
" 3	Ditto, between Fiskum and Fossland	5 Ditto, (30, 28, 25, 16, 5lbs.) rose 8	104	0
" 4	Ditto, near Fossland	2 Ditto, (11, 6lbs.) rose 4	17	0
" 5	Ditto, between Fossland and Fiskum	Caught none! rose 3.		
" 7	Ditto, near Fiskum	2 Salmon, (22, 18lbs.) rose 5	40	0
" 8	Ditto, ditto	Caught none! rose 2 Salmon; 1 Sea-trout	1	8
" 9	Ditto, ditto	4 Salmon, (25, 22, 18, 5lbs.) rose 5	70	0
" 10	Ditto, ditto	1 Ditto; rose 7	18	0
" 11	Ditto, ditto	Caught none! rose none.		
" 12	Ditto, ditto	Ditto 1 rose 1.	21	0
" 14	Ditto, ditto	1 Salmon, (16lbs.) 2 Sea-trout; rose 4 Salmon	34	0
" 15	Ditto, ditto	1 Ditto, rose 5	122	0
" 16	Ditto, between Fiskum and Fossland	6 Ditto, (30, 25, 24, 24, 15, 4lbs.) rose 25	95	8
" 17	Ditto, near Fossland	8 Ditto, (30, 22, 15, 10, 6, 5, 4, 3½lbs.) rose 19	116	0
" 18	Ditto, ditto	6 Ditto, (37, 33, 18, 17, 6, 5lbs.) rose 14	9	0
" 19	Ditto, near Grong	1 Ditto, (6lbs.) 1 Sea-trout (3lbs.) rose 7 Salmon	19	0
" 21	Ditto, ditto	3 Ditto, (11, 4, 4lbs.) rose 13	6	8
" 26	Lake near Hammer	8 Trout	36	0
September 1	River Guul, near Rogstad	2 Salmon, (25, 11lbs.)	42	0
" 2	Ditto, ditto	5 Ditto, (18, 9, 5, 5, 5lbs.)	9	0
" 6	River Hitter, near Brækkan	22 Trout	7	0
" 8	Ditto, near Röraas	12 Ditto	8	0
" 9	River Glommen, near Lake Oresund	7 Ditto		

LIST OF SALMON AND TROUT CAUGHT IN 1839.

WHEN.	WHERE.	WHAT.	Total Wt. lbs.	oz.
May 30	Near Husbyfjöl	10 Trout	14	0
,, 31	Ditto	6 Ditto	15	8
June 16	Beina, near Thomlevolden	1 Ditto	0	4
,, 18	Ditto, near Haave	2 Ditto	1	8
,, 24	Otte Vand	1 Ditto	0	8
,, 25	Gjen-dal	11 Ditto	3	6
,, 26	Near Jerkin	20 Ditto and Grayling	9	8
,, 27	Ditto	30 Ditto ditto	13	0
,, 29	River Guul, near Rogstad	1 Ditto	0	8
July 6	Lake at Hammer, (in 2½ hours)	32 Ditto	18	0
,, 8	Verdals-Elv	1 Salmon	4	8
,, 9	Ditto	5 Trout	5	0
,, 12	River Namsen, near Grong	4 Salmon, (25, 13½, 5, 4lbs.) rose 6	47	8
,, 13	Ditto ditto	11 Ditto, (21, 21, 20, 19, 18, 13, 8, 5, 4, 4, 4lbs.) rose 22	137	0
,, 15	Ditto, near Fossland	3 Ditto, (40, 28, 14lbs.) rose 5	82	0
,, 16	Ditto, near Grong	6 Ditto, (20½, 6, 4, 4, 4, 3) rose 16; 1 Sea-trout, (4lbs.) 1 Common Trout, (1lb.)	44	8
,, 17	Ditto, near Fossland	Did not see a Fish.		
,, 18	Ditto, from Fossland to Fiskum	2 Salmon, (24, 4lbs.) rose 5	28	0
,, 19	Ditto, near Fiskum	5 Ditto, (6, 5, 4, 3, 3lbs.) rose 10	21	0
,, 20	Ditto, ditto	4 Ditto, (22, 5, 4, 4lbs.) rose 4	35	0
,, 22	Ditto, ditto	2 Ditto, (4, 3lbs.) rose 6	7	0
,, 23	Ditto, ditto	8 Ditto, (28, 12, 9, 5, 5, 4, 4, 4lbs.) rose 18	71	0

Month	Day	Location	Catch		
July	24	Ditto, between Fiskum and Fossland	3 Ditto, (13, 4, 4lbs.) rose 8	21	0
,,	25	Ditto, near Fossland	1 Ditto; rose 2	15	0
,,	26	Ditto, near Grong	5 Ditto; rose 13	20	0
,,	27	Ditto, near Værum	9 Ditto, (21, 27, 19, 18, 4, 4, 4, 4lbs.) rose 18	112	0
,,	29	Ditto, near Grong	9 Ditto, (30, 21, 16, 10, 6, 5, 5, 4, 4lbs.) rose 14; 1 Sea-trout, (4lb.)	105	0
,,	30	Ditto, from Grong to Værum	4 Ditto, and 1 Sea-trout; rose 8 Salmon	22	0
August	1	Ditto, near Værum	5 Ditto, (12, 9, 6, 5, 4lbs.) rose 8	36	0
,,	2	Ditto, ditto	2 Ditto, (5, 5lbs.) rose 3	10	0
,,	3	Ditto, near Grong	Caught none! rose 2 small Salmon		
,,	5	Ditto, from Grong to Fiskum	6 Salmon, (27, 18, 11, 6, 4, 3lbs.) rose 13; 1 Sea-trout	69	0
,,	6	Ditto, near Fiskum Foss.	8 Ditto, (30, 18, 17, 16, 16, 12, 5, 4lbs.) rose 13	118	0
,,	7	Ditto, below Fiskum	4 Ditto, (22, 18, 16, 4lbs.) rose 13	60	0
,,	8	Ditto, near Fiskum Foss.	9 Ditto, (27, 20, 19, 16, 5, 5, 4, 4, 4lbs.) rose 14	104	0
,,	9	Ditto, ditto	2 Ditto, (10, 3lbs.) rose 5	13	0
,,	10	Ditto, ditto	3 Ditto, (24, 17, 11lbs.) rose 6; 1 Sea-trout	55	0
,,	12	Ditto, ditto	11 Ditto, (37, 34, 33, 24, 23, 18, 18, 11, 10, 4, 4lbs.) rose 18	216	0
,,	13	Ditto, from Fiskum to Fossland	4 Ditto, (21, 16, 12, 4lbs.) rose 9; 2 Sea-trout	56	8
,,	14	Ditto, near Fiskum Foss.	4 Ditto, (34, 31, 20, 18lbs.) rose 4	103	0
,,	15	Ditto, below Fiskum	7 Ditto, (25, 21, 19, 18, 5, 4, 4lbs.) rose 16; 1 Sea-trout	97	0
,,	16	Ditto, ditto	2 Ditto, (6, 3lbs.) rose 7	9	0
,,	17	Ditto, ditto	Caught none! rose 2 small Salmon		
,,	19	Ditto, from Fiskum to Grong	3 Salmon, (26, 18, 4lbs.) rose 9	48	0
,,	21	Ditto, near Fossland	2 Ditto, (4, 4lbs.) rose 6; 1 Sea-trout	9	8
,,	29	River Örke, near Moe	1 Sea-trout; 1 Common ditto	2	0
September	2	River Rauma, near Veblungsnaes	1 Salmon	8	0
,,	4	Ditto, ditto	1 Ditto	21	0
,,	9	Lessöe Lake and River	40 Trout and Grayling, (7, 3, 2, 2lbs., &c.)	26	0
,,	12	Near Hund in Biri	5 Trout	0	10

RELATIVE VALUE OF MONEY, WEIGHTS, AND MEASURES.

HAMBURG MONEY.

16 Skillings .... =1 Mark.
3 Marks.......... =1 Hamburg Dollar.
3 Marks 12 Skillings=1 Specie Thaler.

An English Sovereign is usually equal to about 17 marks; therefore, an English penny equals about 1¼ Hamburg skilling.

DANISH MONEY.

16 Skillings =1 Mark.
6 Marks.. =1 Rigsbank daler (paper.)
12 Marks.. =1 Specie Rigsdaler (silver.)

An English Sovereign is usually equal to about 9 Rigsbank dalers : therefore, an English penny equals about 3½ Danish skillings.

SWEDISH MONEY.

48 Skillings ... =1 Rix daler.

2^x Banco .... $=3^x$ Rix.

48 Skillings b^{co.}=1 Rix daler b^{co.}=72 Skillings Rixgeld.

48 Skillings rix=1 Rix daler (rix)=32 Skillings Banco.

An English Sovereign is usually equal to about 11 dalers 32 skillings Rix : therefore, an English penny equals about 2¼ skillings Banco, or 3¼ skillings Rix.

———

NORWEGIAN MONEY.

24 Skillings=1 Mark, or Ort, as it is called in the North.

5 Marks.. =1 Daler.

An English Sovereign is usually equal to 5 dalers : therefore, an English penny equals about 2¼ Norwegian skillings.

The above relations to English values must of course vary with the rates of exchange : I have given what were the average values during my recent visits; they will be found sufficiently accurate for all ordinary purposes.

NORWEGIAN MEASURES OF WEIGHTS.

2 Lods .=1 Ounce.

2 Marks.=1 Pound.

12 Pounds=1 Bismal Pund (often called simply " a Pund.")

16 Pounds=1 Lispund.

36 Pounds=1 Vog.

320 Pounds=1 Skippund.

100 Pounds Norwegian=109,869lbs. avoirdupois English.

SCANDINAVIAN MEASURES OF LENGTH.

Danish   Mile= 8,244 English yds. =4.684 British stat. miles.

Swedish   do.=11,700   ditto   =6.640   ditto.

Norwegian do.=12,352   ditto   =7.180 . ditto.

The Norwegian mile is equal to 18,000 ells, or 36,000 feet: the Norwegian and the Rhenish foot are the same.

1000 feet Norwegian are equal to 1029.36 feet English: the Encyclopædia Britannica gives 1000 feet Norwegian, equal to 1033 feet English; but from the authority I had for my statement, I believe it to be the most correct. According to the Edinburgh Cabinet Library, the Norwegian (or Rhenish) ell is equal to 24.71 British imperial inches ; which would make 1000 feet Norwegian, equal to 1028 feet English, nearly.

According to the Edinburgh Encyclopædia the Swedish ell is equal to 23.37 British imperial inches. And, finally, according to the semi-official map of the roads in Sweden and Norway, published at Stockholm by Brandenburg, in 1831, the Swedish mile is said to be to the Norwegian in the proportion of 1 : 1.0572. The discrepancies among the above authorities prove that they cannot be depended on for scientific calculations : but they are probably all sufficiently near the truth for the Tourist's information.

It, perhaps, may be interesting, as serving to convey some idea of the accommodations to be expected in the better kind of Norwegian Inn, as well as of the prices, if I subjoin a copy of the Tariff, established for the district North of Trondhjem; and which will be found nearly similar to those fixed for other rural parts of Norway. These lists being official, a severe penalty is attached to their infraction: and as they are ordered to be affixed in a conspicuous place in the Traveller's apartment, it is his own fault if he be greatly overcharged.

" List of Prices established for North Trondhjem's Amt,
August, 1836, *by Fogman*, *G. Matthesen*.

For Personer uden for Almuestanden.

Skillings.

For Værelse, med Lys, Varme, og Seng, per Dogn	16
„ Værelse med Seng, uden Lys og Varme	10
„ een ret varm Mad, med Bröd til	12
„ een ret kold Mad, eller een Portion Smörre-bröd, med Ost, og Kjöd, eller deslige	8
„ een Contoir-kop god Kaffee, med Flöde, og Sukker	6
„ een Contoir-kop god Congo thee, med ditto . .	3
„ een Flaske, eller een Potte godt, stærkere end almindeligt, Æl.	4
„ een Flaske, eller een Potte almindeligt Æl	2
„ Dram godt Fransk Brændeviin.	2
„ Dram godt Fransk Brændeviin, Karve-aquavit	2
„ Dram godt Norsk Brændeviin, à 6 Grader. . . .	1

For Personer af Almuestanden.

For Værelse, med Seng, Lys, og Varme, per Dogn 6
,, Værelse, med Seng, uden Lys og Varme 2

Forlanger den Reisende særdeles Beværtning af Mad og
Drikkevarer, betales derfor efter Overeenskomft. Foranforte
Taxt gjælder indtil videre.

Translation of the above Tariff

List of Prices to be paid by persons above the common rank.

Skillings.

For apartment, with lights, fire, and bed, per diem,
    (a day and a night) 16
,, Apartment with bed, but without lights or fire 10
,, a good warm meal, with bread to it 12
,, a good cold meal, or a portion of bread and but-
    ter, with cheese or meat, or the like 8
,, a large cup of good coffee, with cream and sugar 6
,, ditto   congo tea, with ditto 3
,, for a bottle or pot of good ale, stronger than or-
    dinary 4
,, ditto, of common ale.................... 2
,, a glass of good French brandy 2
,, ditto of aquavitæ, flavoured with caraway 2
,, ditto good Norwegian brandy, of 6 degrees (of
    strength) 1

Prices for Persons of the lower orders.

For apartment with bed, light, and fire, per diem.. 6
,, ditto   ditto   without lights and fire.... 2

Should the traveller require any particular service of eatables
or liquors, they must be paid for according to private agreement.

The above Tariff is in force until further notice.

If the reader will refer to a former table for the value of a Norwegian skilling, he will see there can be no reason to complain of the exorbitance of this list of prices. He must not, however, think that he can readily obtain every one of the above articles by expressing his readiness to pay for them. The third and fourth articles, for instance, will almost invariably, resolve themselves into nothing better than "a portion of bread and butter, with cheese or the like." Very seldom indeed will he get "a good warm or cold meal of meat:" and the "French brandy," he will soon find, was never out of Norway.

I have added a vocabulary of some words and phrases likely to prove most useful to the Traveller either on the road, or at the inn: he may find it more convenient, than to have to search for the words he wants in a dictionary. It will at least serve for a commencement, which I should strongly recommend him to improve and increase by as large an acquaintance with the language itself, as his time and aptitude for foreign tongues will allow.

Nothing is so great a comfort and advantage as to be, at least in some degree, acquainted with the language of the country in which one is travelling. Each step of progress in it amply compensates for the labour bestowed: and Norsk, in particular, is so easy in its construction, and withal so like English, that our countrymen at any rate cannot find it difficult. It is said, with justice, to bear a still closer resemblance to Lowland Scotch : and in attempting to speak it, I should recommend the stranger to endeavour to imitatè the broad accent, and the slow, singsong delivery of the Scottish Lowlander, rather than the rapid, indistinct, closemouthed pronunciation of many of the higher classes of Englishmen.

The vowels have the broad open sound, given them by every people, except ourselves : the final *e* is always sounded, but is usually short. When *o* has two dots over it, as thus, *ö*, it is pronounced like the French diphthong *œ* in *œil*. When *a* has the same two dots, as thus, *ä*, it has the long sound of our *a*, in "*case*," for instance. The double *aa* sounds exactly like our *oa* ; thus, *Aar*, the Year, is pronounced as our *Oar*. The vowel *y* is pronounced nearly like the French *u* : while the Norwegian *j* has the sound and power of our consonantic *y*.

The consonants require little remark ; except perhaps that *d*, where it follows a consonant, seems, in general, only to increase the sound of the preceding consonant thus, *Fjelder*, Mountains, is pronounced *Fyel-ler:* where it commences a syllable, it has its usual sound. The accents are very various : and no intelligible description of them, or directions for their employment, can easily be given.

The Norsk verbs and substances have as few and simple inflections, as can well be. The regular verbs take a final *r* in the three persons singular of the

present tense; otherwise they end in *e* throughout
the active voice; and do not vary, either for person
or number. In the passive voice they assume a
final *s*, in addition to the corresponding tense of the
active: the auxiliary verbs are very similar to ours,
both in sound and use. Thus, *jeg* (pronounced *yei*)
elsker, I love; *han,* or *hun, elsker,* he or she loves;
vi elske, de elske, we, they, love. *Jeg elskede,* I
loved: *Jeg skal elske,* I shall love. And in the
passive, *Jeg,* or *de, elskes,* I, or they, are loved: *jeg
elskedes,* I was loved: *Jeg skal elskes,* I shall be loved.

Where there is any difference between the singular
and plural of substantives, the latter is commonly
formed by the addition of *e,* or *er:* the genitive takes
a final *s,* or the proposition *af* (of) as in English:
the other cases have no inflection.

But by far the greatest peculiarity of the Norsk
language is the use of the articles: these are *en* for
the masculine and feminine; *et,* for the neuter gender.
When prefixed, they constitute the indefinite article;
when added as a termination to a substantive, they
become the definite: *ne* is the universal definite article
of the plural. Thus, *Hest,* horse; *en Hest,* a horse;
Hesten, the horse: *Hester,* horses; *Hesterne,* the
horses: *Hestens,* of the horse; *Hesternes,* of the
horses. But when an adjective is joined with the
substantive, the demonstrative pronoun (*den, det, de*)
is employed as the definite article: as thus, *den
hvide Hest,* the white horse; *det sorte Haar,* the
black hair: *de hvide Hester,* the white horses.

The collocation of the words in a sentence follows the English construction, as nearly as possible : but I believe it will be found the best plan, in this as in all other languages, for the beginner to content himself with pronouncing, as distinctly as he can, the substantive that expresses the idea of what he wants. He is thus much more likely to make himself understood, than if he attempt to form a perfectly correct grammatical sentence ; and thereby run the chance of perplexing his hearer by so many more words improperly pronounced.

The written language of Norway, as also the language of the pulpit, the stage, and the best society, is precisely the same as the Danish ; though the pronunciation is considerably different. The dialects in Norway vary very much ; in consequence, doubtless, of the little communication that the inhabitants of their confined vallies have with each other. It may however, be said generally, that wherever the patois of the peasants differ from pure Danish, they approach so much nearer to the Swedish. The latter is so like Norsk, that intelligent natives of the two countries can mutually understand each other : but it is much more harmonious to the ear ; indeed, to my taste, when agreeably spoken, as it often is by the Swedish ladies, it is, next to Italian, the sweetest language I ever heard. Many of the harsher Norwegian sounds are softened down. The vowel e is frequently changed into a : k, which in Norsk is pronounced hard (except in a few rare instances where it precedes *j*) is in Swedish always soft whenever it precedes a soft vowel (*e, i, ö.*) Thus *Kinnekulle,* is pronounced *Chinne koolle,* &c.

I proceed now to give a short catalogue of some of the most useful words for the Tourist in Norway.

Carriole....	Name of the Norwegian one-horse carriage.	Trikke-penge,	Drink money.
		Koffert	Portmanteau.
		Kasse......	Box.
Vogn	Carriage in general	Foderal	Case.
Hjul, (pronounced Hyool) Wheel.			
Armene	The Shafts.	Middag-mad,	Dinner.
Tomme	Rein.	Nat-mad ..	Supper.
Sele	Harness.	Frokost	Breakfast.
Svöbe, (in Swedish, Piskan) Whip.		Noget til spise,	Something to eat.
Fjeder	Spring.	Kjöd	Fresh meat.
Smör	Grease.	Flesk	Salt meat.
Skydskaffer .	Man that supplies post horses.	Vild	Game.
		Fugl	Bird.
Skydskarl ..	Boy that goes with horses.	Rensdyr....	Reindeer.
		Tihür	Capercailzie.
Tilsigelsepenge,	Money paid for ordering the horses: 4 sks. for each.	Urhan	Black cock.
		Rype	Ptarmigan.
		Hjerpe	Hasel hen.
		Fisk ...,...	Fish.
Skiftet	The Stage.	Skinke	Ham, or Bacon.
Gastgivergaard,	Inn.	Sild	Herring.
Dagbog....	Daybook, in which the Traveller must enter his name, &c	Ægger	Eggs.
		Potata	Potatoes.
		Smörre bröd,	Bread and Butter
Päpir	Paper.	Gammel Ost,	Old Cheese.
Penne......	Pen.	Flad bröd ..	Flat bread, or Barley cake.
Blække	Ink.		

Melk . . . . . . Milk.
Flöde . . . . . . Cream.
Sukker . . . . Sugar.
Smör . . . . . . Butter.
Thee . . . . . . Tea.
Kaffee . . . . Coffee.
En Dram Brandtviin, A glass of Brandy.
Bord . . . . . . Table.
Stul . . . . . . Chair.
Kniv . . . . . . Knife.
Gaffel . . . . . . Fork.
Skee . . . . . . Spoon.
Tellerken . . Plate.
Kopp . . . . . . Cup.
Stor Glæs . . Large Glass.
Kasserolle . . Kettle.
Stege-pande, Fryingpan.
Ild . . . . Fire (the element).
Varme . . . . Fire (in room).
Nat quartier, Night lodging.
Værelse . . . . Room, or Chamber
Seng . . . . . . Bed.
Lagene . . . . The Sheets.
Teppe . . . . Coverlid.
Lys . . . . . . Lights, or Candle.
Vindue . . . . Window.
Dören . . . . The Door.
Vaske bolle . Washing basin.
Vand (vulgar, Vatten) Water.
Haandklæd . Towel.
Sæbe . . . . . . Soap.
Regningen . . The Bill.
Gode Betaling, Good Pay.
Mand . . . . . . Husband.
Kone . . . . . . Wife.

Sön . . . . Son.
Datter . . . . Daughter.
Dreng . . . . . . Boy.
Pige . . . . . . Girl.
Liden God, (familiar for) Little Child.
Börn . . . . . . Children.
Tjener . . . . Servant.
Tolk . . . . . . Interpreter.
Frak . . . . . . Coat.
Beenklæder . Trowsers.
Hut . . . . . . Hat.
Lue . . . . . . Cap.
Lomme . . . . Pocket.

Hest . . . . . . Horse.
Hengst . . . . Stallion.
Hoppe, or Mære, Mare.
Halt . . . . . . Lame.
Ingen Sko paa, No Shoe on.
Veien . . . . . . The Road.
Bakke . . . . Hill.
Fjeld . . . . . . Mountain range.
Bjerg . . . . . . Rock.
Fjord . . . . . . Arm of the Sea.
Elv . . . . . . River.
Næs (properly Nose) hence a Promontory.
Vand (used often for Lake) properly Water.
Söe . . . . Lake, generally large.
Færge . . . . . . Ferry.
Foss . . . . . . Waterfall.
Mark . . . . . . Field, or cultivated Land.

Ager	Cornfield.	Snelle	Reel.
Eng	Meadow.	Angel, or Krog, Hook.
Hvede	Wheat.	Flue	Fly.
Ryg	Rye.	Flu-angel, or	
Byg	Barley.	Flue-krog }	Artificial fly.
Havre	Oats.	Lax	Salmon.
Græs	Grass.	Öret, or Örred, Trout.
Hö	Hay.	Syk	Grayling.
Lade	Barn.	Gjedde	Pike.
Creatur	Cattle.	Aborre	Perch.
Hund	Dog.	Gorkin	Bleak.
Sviin	Pig.	Naat, or Næt, Large Drawing
Sætter	Summer pasturage		Net.
Skov	Wood, or Forest.	Garn	Smaller Net, usu-
Træ	(piece of) Wood;		ally fixed.
	also, Tree.	Idag	To-day.
Ask	Ash.	Igaar	Yesterday.
Birk	Birch.	Imorgen	To-morrow.
Fyrü	Scotch Fir.	Tidlig	Early.
Gran	Spruce.	Seen	Late.
Gaard	Farm house.	Iquell	In the Evening.
Præstegaard,	Priest's Residence.	Klokken, to, tre, Two, three
By	Town (from which		o'clock.
	the termination of	Dyb	Deep.
	so many English	Grund	Shallow.
	places is derived.)	Færdig	Ready.
Landet	The Country.	Langsom	Slow.
Björn	Bear.	Reen	Clean.
Ræve	Fox.	Smudsig	Dirty.
Ulv	Wolf.	Ingen	No one.
Baad	Boat (sound nearly	Intet	Nothing.
	the same.)	Ikke	Not.
Aare	Oar (ditto).	Nei	No.
Roerskarl	Rower.	Ja, (jo, in answer to a negative)
Fiske-stang	Fishing-rod.		Yes.
Fiske-snur	Fishing-line.	Mange	Many.

Meget......	Much.		Hvile	to rest.
Noget	Something.		Ligge	to lie down.
Strax	Immediately.		Sove	to sleep.
Snart	Quickly.		Stege	to fry.
Fort!	Get on!		Koge	to boil.
Tilbage	Back again.		Slaae	to strike.
Höjere Haand,	Right hand.		Skee	to happen.
Venstre Haand	Left hand.		Sætte paa ..	to put on (the fire &c.)
Kan	Can.			
Vil	Will.		God dag....	Good day.
Skal	Shall.		Adje Farvel .	Goodbye, farewell.
Maa	Must.		Vär so god, at,	Be so good as to
Faae	to get.		Om Forladse,	I beg your pardon.
Skaffe	to procure.		Komm hiit!	Come here!
Raabe......	to call.		Giv mig min,	Give me my
Hente......	to fetch.		Lukke Dören til,	Shut the door.
Springe	to run, or jump.		Aabne Vinduen,	Open the window.
Reise	to travel.			

Jeg takker Mange Tak	Thank you. Many thanks.
Tak skal De have	Thanks shall you have.
Godt Veir	Good weather.
Regn Veir	Rainy weather.
Slem Vei	Bad road.
Bedste Slags	The best kind.
Det blæser	It blows hard.
Hvörlēdĕs befinder De Dem?	How do you do?
Hvem hedder Du!	What is your name?
Hvad kales dette?	What is that called?
Jeg forstaaer ikke	I do not understand.
Jeg er en Fremmed, en Engelskemand,	I am a stranger, an Englishman.
Jeg kan ikke tale Norsk	I cannot speak Norwegian.
Du maa tale langsom	You must speak slowly.
Hvad koster det?	What does that cost?

Hvor langt er det herfra til ..	How far is it from here to
Er denne Veien til.........	Is this the road to
Hvor mange Klokken er det ?	What o'clock is it ?
Er der Ingen hjemme ?......	Is there no one at home ?
Kan jeg ligge her ?.........	Can I sleep here ?
Kan jeg faae noget til spise ?..	Can I get any thing to eat ?
Hvor ere Hesterne?	Where are the horses ?
Hesterne vare bestilt om Klokken eet	The horses were ordered for one o'clock.
Hvor er min Tjener ?........	Where is my servant ?
Hvor mange Aar gammel er Du ?	How old are you ?
Kjærre paa-or, frem !	Drive on !
Giv mig Regningen	Give me the bill.
Findes ingen Baad her ?	Is there no boat here ?
Kan man skaffe mig en Baad, med et Par Roerskarl ..	Can you procure me a boat, with a couple of rowers ?
Kan jeg faae en Hest strax ?..	Can I get a horse directly ?
Nok een til...............	One more.

NUMERALS.

Een	1	Tretten...............	13
To	2	Fjorten..............	14
Tre	3	Femten..............	15
Fier	4	Sexten	16
Fem	5	Sytten	17
Sex	6	Atten	18
Syv	7	Nitten	19
Otte	8	Tyve.................	20
Ni...................	9	Een og tyve	21
Ti...................	10	To og tyve	22
Elleve	11	Tredive..............	30
Tolv	12	Fyrretyve	40

Halvtresindstyve, or briefly Halvtreds	} 50	Fjersindstyve	80
Tresindstyve	60	Halvfemsindstyve or Halvfems	} 90
Halvfjersindstyve, or Halvfjers	} 70	Hundrede	100

Den förste .... The first   Den tredie .... The third
Den anden .... The second   Den fjerde.... The fourth, &c.

Den förste gang, The first time. Den anden gang, The second time.

Een gang .... Once.   To gang...... Twice.
Tre gang .... Thrice.

The Norwegian method of reckoning fractions of time or distances, is rather puzzling to a stranger at first : thus, "Klokken er halv tre;" means, it is half past two o'clock ; or, *half way from the last number towards three.* So also " halv tresindstyve," signifies that it is *half way from the last number forty, towards three times twenty,* or sixty ; that is, it is fifty : and so on, with the others.

If the stage be a mile and a half, you may perhaps be told that it is "halv anden miil ;" or *half way towards the second mile :* but more probably, that it is " Sex fjerding," or six quarters. If the distance be half a mile and an eighth, they will call it "fem ottendeel," or five eighths. A slight acquaintance with vulgar fractions will render this simple to the

Traveller: but should he be told that the stage is "halv sex Fjerding;" he must not fancy it to be only three quarters, or *the half of six*: he will find it to be five quarters, and an eighth; or *half way from five towards six*, upon the same principle as before explained.

THE END.

Pardon, Printer, Alfred Place, Blackfriars Road.

Lightning Source UK Ltd.
Milton Keynes UK
UKHW020735140922
408851UK00005B/534